NICOLA, MILAN

SEMIOTEXT(E) NATIVE AGENTS SERIES

© 2014 Lodovico Pignatti Morano

Published by Semiotext(e)
2007 Wilshire Blvd., Suite 427, Los Angeles, CA 90057
www.semiotexte.com

Special thanks to Robert Dewhurst and Carlye Packer.

Cover Art: Reena Spaulings, *A Place in the Sun (Shadows) 12,* 2009.
Inkjet and lithograph. 36 x 24 inches.
Courtesy of Campoli Presti, London/Paris.

Back Cover Photography: Lodovico Pignatti Morano
Design: Hedi El Kholti

ISBN: 978-1-58435-128-3
Distributed by The MIT Press, Cambridge, Mass. and London, England
Printed in the United States of America

NICOLA, MILAN

Lodovico Pignatti Morano

Thanks to:

Amy Lien
Richard Verde
John Dine

1

I arrive in New York from San Francisco, on a quick stop before going back to Milan. In my hotel, which is better than the kind in which I usually stay, there is an enormous world map cut out from cast iron attached to the wall behind the reception desk, dimly illuminated from behind. I'm speaking to the lady behind the desk with a curt knowingness I can only use overseas, but I'm distracted and really looking up at this map. The lack of motion it expresses distresses me, the dumb muteness, completely fake, obviously an enormous joke—it's a shock to my sense of self to have such a thing served up to me on a plate like that.

I laugh it off gently as I get into the lift, holding firm, my body not moving too far towards my emotions.

After my brief visit to New York it's time to go back to Milan. For the last three days my cheeks have been permanently red as if all the sugar I've eaten on the trip has been cooked up in a heat of nervousness and caramelized and is now cracking on the surface of my face. I've been masking my stink of nerves all day every day for the entire trip in coffee and a horse-hide leather jacket which is fifty years old but still smells—on this last evening I try to come off it all, the constant coffee, with three quick beers—I feel them in my head, trying to relax my blood, for a moment the caffeine and alcohol mix in a high pitched fever—I'm shaky, sick feeling, paranoid—I still can't shake the paranoia of illness abroad—then the fevered moment passes and I begin to relax into the reward of great fatigue.

In Milan, in the weeks before I left for the trip, the part of my mind that thinks while I sleep had quietly been insisting that I had become something else—I'd been waking up thinking strange thoughts to myself, thoughts claiming some kind of authority to speak, speak as a country or of it, as if I knew something about it—not that I knew anything about it at all. "I am the company," I'd wake up saying some mornings. It was the time of year right before the clocks got wound back an hour and the mornings had quite suddenly become very dark, so these thoughts seemed to occur in an exaggerated quiet, as if to heighten the feeling that nobody would ever notice what had happened to me.

That's why I'd gone there, though, as far as I could remember, to Milan. To that empty city. To a city that exists only as much as the name of a city stamped on luxury brand shopping bags exists. I'd gone with that explicit intention—to steal someone or something's cultural authority.

When we land in Milan it's dusk. I've been away long enough to not know what to expect from the weather. I take off my sweater and step out onto the steps in a t-shirt, the cool evening air drifts up between the cotton and my stomach, chest, and armpits making me feel even skinnier and younger.

I look around, the dusk seems to surround us in a 180-degree arc, across the length of my vision, the hills that enclose the airport seem to be glowing in every direction.

Everybody steps off the plane and walks down the staircase quietly, two fashion ladies behind me speak in low voices, a young middle class couple in front of me stare at each other with their faces close together, their eyes a little moist.

"This is a chosen land," I say to myself under my breath. The expression escapes before I even know what I'm saying.

I look at all the Italian passengers. They must think that this land is theirs when they look at it, that some inexplicable fate ties them to it. When they come back from overseas and are greeted by this slow hushed glow of land murmuring in all directions they must think that they belong to it, that it is their natural destiny to follow the rhythms of the place until their deaths.

"What a simple unraveling."

I feel like I barely exist, mingling amongst these people.

I hold onto the rail on the bus and sway slightly as it drives in strange curves across the tarmac towards the arrivals area. I realize that momentarily we're going to have to go inside the terminal and I will no longer be able to contemplate the dusk. I grasp at the last moments of observation offered by the scene. My calm blankness is not interrupted. I slide quickly off the bus and into the terminal, through customs with my small bag in hand and out to the other side of the airport. I have no idea what I'm going to do next.

2

The wooden motorboat slides through a tight quiet canal in Venice. Nicola, one of the three men on the boat, places a pair of large sleek frameless and futuristic sunglasses on Danny's face, a transsexual ex-back-up dancer for Grace Jones who he has hired for the night. She has very pale skin and a quiff dyed white-blonde, gelled back into a sort of biomorphic ripple, though her eyes are banally revealing. They seem to belong to another version of her, one that reveals her origins— suburban, teenage, wounded, aspirational, ironic—so typical of their time.

But Nicola puts the sunglasses on her face and covers these banal eyes. The effect of the enormous frames on the dancer's head (they make her look a bit like a sort of aggressively hard-bodied homage to Peggy Guggenheim) is not at all surprising to him—the look is more or less identical to that which he had imagined when he purchased the glasses a month ago in a sleepy town just outside a bigger city, a place where he'd found a strangely gifted artisan, a bedroom artisan (a kid, basically, who still lived at home but had found some way to dream with his hands, short circuiting, like the internet, one culture to another geography) who could make up these sorts of things according to Nicola's particular, articulate requests.

He was right to cover her eyes, he thinks, but without any sense of surprise—he doesn't really make mistakes with these kinds of things anymore.

He, Nicola, is bald-headed, but at thirty or thirty-one, the youngest and obviously most powerful of the three men on the boat. After placing the sunglasses on Danny's face he walks back and stands near the photographer, a little behind him, pretending to not notice exactly what's going on though he occasionally, discreetly, checks the screen of the camera to make sure the images are coming out as he wants.

You can imagine it took him awhile to figure out how to style his hair when it started falling out. He was used to being a long-haired student, probably, placing his palms on his temples and burying his fingers in the thick strands near his crown as he studied endlessly in the library—he used to be the kind of student people called a wunderkind—when he thought, he thought feverishly. Those days are brutally long gone now, or so it appears. Now he has learnt how to wear it, the balding scalp, in an almost mildewy not-crewcut version of very short, maybe cut only with scissors to keep the acerbic edge off it, in the art of the nonstatement, or the statement which if you're good enough at making, can become entirely irrelevant, and so give you the freedom to do whatever you want. He usually dresses the same way, with a kind of snobbism so extreme it can't manifest itself even in dress, a defeated all-knowingness, an extremely expensive defeat, with a particular expertise in fabrics, in the kinds of details that convey nothing to the inexpert eye. But a strange speed-bump remains about Nicola's hair, as if losing it was disproportionately difficult, completely unlike the ease with which he discredits all but the most cunning logic now. He always has something to say about a friend's haircut.

"How much do they make you pay for a job like that?"

"€20."

"€20? You can get sucked off for that money."

"Yeah and I can jerk myself off for free."

The hair on his face, though, is still spiky and razored, and his chest is hairy, from one end to the other. There is not much he can do about that.

That night at his party in Venice, he looks at his absolute best.

He's wearing a white suit, it probably cost a million euros. It's the only one he has and he wears it every time he feels it's a special occasion. At least that's the impression it gives. Underneath he's wearing a sheer white t-shirt with a watercolor-like pattern across it, cut very deep down the chest … something designer, innocuous, expensive, unreal, inasmuch as it's the kind of the thing you'd only buy for a night like this and nights like these are barely known to exist. It matches his suit perfectly. Around his neck he has a necklace made of many rings of extremely heavy raw-looking steel of different thicknesses. The way he wears it makes one wonder how his expertise can be so vast and all encompassing. His eyes are done in a thick smoky blue.

He put this make-up of his on earlier, by himself, in a private hotel room he hired just to get dressed.

He'd arrived with a small tube-shaped nylon gym bag. In it he had his suit, gently rolled to avoid too many wrinkles, his t-shirt, jewelery, new shoes, and cosmetics. Even though the heavy curtains were closed a little bit of light seeped in; that sadly impersonal light of hot mid-afternoon, a few minutes before three when everything is about to reopen.

Standing near the bed he took off all the clothes he was wearing. Then he went to the bathroom with his make-up. The bathroom was large, with a heavy marble sink. Everything in it was either brown or cream or pinkish red; it almost made him drowsy and momentarily he thought about sleep with great pleasure even though the evening was still very distant.

Then he did what he'd gone in there thinking to do; he looked at himself in the mirror and smiled, first with his eyebrows and then with his mouth. The smile, though pre-meditated, had the effect of making him want to continue smiling. He tried various different effects. His eyes shone ever so lightly and he filled them with even more of their own color, so they seemed like stones.

Then he started to apply his make-up, meticulously, slowly—already knowing the effect he was after—it had occurred to him a few days ago as he slowly arrived at this outfit in his mind. As if working in metaphor—for what, he didn't know—he'd begun layering one part of the look onto another, as if coming home, arriving at the image he knew he wanted to live in that night.

He applied a light grey foundation under his eyes, then an ultramarine blue, then a light electric blue, gradually the slightly oily one-day-old feeling of depth that he sought.

When he'd finished, he put all his other clothes and toiletries into the gym bag. He gave the bag to the man behind the front desk, who was a sort of friend, or at least someone willing to do him a favor, and told him he would be back early tomorrow morning to pick it up.

He arrived at the dock empty handed and entirely prepared, as though he was an image rather than somebody on a night out with friends.

The other men in the motorboat, the men with whom Nicola has decided to surround himself, are dressed with a similar sense of occasion, old hands at putting on a show, confident in their ability to incite a spectacle in a few hours when the party starts.

Both men, in their late forties or early fifties, treat Nicola familiarly, as if he were an old friend even though they can't have known each other much longer than a year, eighteen months at the most. In fact, though it's almost imperceptible—invisible to the untrained eye—there's something a little too fast about their familiarity, as if it were afraid to really settle on its object. When Fabio, the photographer for the evening and the jumpier of the two men, says something about the photos he's taking of Danny at the rear of the boat, he seems to rush his comment past Nicola, to make it willfully imprecise, as though afraid of what might happen if it directly hit its target. Nicola smiles back reassuringly, gently allowing Fabio's nervous conceit.

The other man, a little older, a little more dangerous-looking, with a head like one you might find on a Greek sculpture representing some wicked and eternally boyish mythological character, watches on. He is dressed in a manner that seems to use the stylistic tropes of homosexuality as a threat, to other men, heterosexuals mostly, of rape. He is wearing a sarong-like designer piece, perhaps originally for women, with a blazer jacket. On his head he wears a platinum blonde wig tied back into a pony tail and 70s-style gold wire framed glasses.

The motorboat eventually exits the narrow canals and cruises to the dock on the Riva degli Schiavoni where the larger cruise boat on which the party will be held is waiting. Even though the party won't begin for another few hours, they board immediately and go straight to the open-air top floor. A couple of tattooed men are setting up the bar behind the counter at the fore of the boat, next to the small open cabin.

Nicola and his friends greet them familiarly with a series of more or less jokey handshakes. Inside the small cabin a thin boy is checking the sound system. Nicola greets him as well, shaking the boy's hand and softly gripping his forearm at the same time, as if happy to have him in his hands, quite literally. Then he smiles and says:

"Play just as if it were a normal night for you in Mexico City, I want the same atmosphere, okay?"

He doesn't describe what he means in any more detail though the Mexico City he wants to hear in the music is a specific one, nightmarish and mythic.

The kid, who is young and smooth-skinned and wearing a black t-shirt with white gothic drawings and Spanish text, smiles mischievously, touching his mouth with the back of his hand, as if he thinks Nicola is a real joker but he doesn't mind right now—he'll tolerate it this time because the guy paid for his flight over, though maybe in other circumstances he wouldn't put up with it. He responds:

"Mexico City … Yeah yeah yeah no problem. Just like Mexico City, okay, heh."

Nicola laughs a little to himself as he notices the kid's need to express, somehow, even if just for a fraction of a second in the corner of his lips or eyes, his independence, his freedom of will. Nicola laughs because that's fine, in fact he likes it, it's perfect, it's exactly what he expected and wanted, that guy shouldn't like him.

The men who were setting up the bar finish and seem to say something to one of Nicola's friends who proceeds to help himself to a drink, the night's first. Gradually the others notice and prepare themselves some simple cocktails. They all stand together, talking quietly and enjoying the feeling of their nerves mixing together in the air, recognizing the sense of anticipation like a familiar friend; they've done this a million times before because it's their favorite thing to do.

He's only the hype man for the party that night but Nicola steals the show. After about an hour, after the first effects of the vodka can be felt on the crowd, Danny, specifically hired for this moment, steps up onto the bar table and begins an aggressive striptease. She is then joined by a girl who also begins stripping and sexually engaging Danny.

The crowd, a mix of bored rich people who pay, with base hunger, to have a city's "secrets" revealed (in an attempt to breach the horrifically deadening sense of never being anywhere specific, no matter what city they're in), and the best-looking creative kids from various Italian cities, has enough of an innate sense of entitlement to leer at the show without scruples when they feel like it, and act as if it weren't happening at all when they don't feel like it.

Nicola stands directly behind the two dancers entreating the crowd to engage with the performance, shouting at them to "lose themselves" amongst other similarly self-evident exhortations. He continues to repeat them, rhythmically, like a chant, with greater and greater force—his intensity is hard to believe, disproportionate to his cunning intelligence. His face is a spectacle of incredibly base sensations, passing through it one after the other: hatred, power, fear. It's impossible to understand what his face means to him in those moments. It's impossible not to look at him.

Occasionally he takes a break from his exhortations and comes downstairs to the aft of the boat to see a woman, his wife (though he never uses the term). She is tall, with extremely short hair and a face that seems as though it's been beaten before, but her eyes are so calmly assertive that they make this observation seem like a deliciously fantastic paranoia … it has a slightly irregular puffiness, a bit out of shape in unexpected areas. He smiles at her with what appears to be straightforward sincerity, kisses her briefly on the cheek, then goes back upstairs to continue his performance.

He gets behind the bar and begins shouting again. He is sweating a little, not a lot, not as much as you'd expect, but enough to cake his make-up into an even more glamorous sheen; it makes him look like he's at the tail end of a bender, that he's been wearing that painted face for four days straight—that he's already passed through one of those nights where you stay up through until dawn and when dawn comes you realize that sleep won't be coming to you that next day because the situation demands vigilance, you're on the cusp of something, if you keep watching you'll catch them or it, one of those periods without sleep, basically, where you finally decide to leave something behind.

He continues his performance for a further twenty or so minutes.

Even though he acknowledges the crowd, and in a way entirely relies on it for whatever feeling he is trying to achieve, his satisfaction remains deeply private, darkly so, disconnected from the performance and from what he's giving the audience. You can tell from the look in his eyes; he's not anybody's friend. The look seems to be saying "you'll never know the origin of this desire." He'll never "share" anything with you— and this adds to the flavor of things, that he'll never tell anyone what it meant to him. It's a kind of secret literature in action, one that people refuse to write anymore, one that here, seemingly, nobody ever talks about.

3

I went to his party in Venice and even kept the invitation, a strange small business card, in my wallet until much later—I met other people too, who had kept it, when they looked for an evasive €5 note or business card it would spill out of their over-stretched wallets, a hard, glinting treasure.

It was an exciting object, the invite. The words on it were chilling and true but you couldn't imagine how anyone could have possibly chosen them, over all the other words in the world. The same could be said for images in the patterned background. The card was articulate in a perfectly complicated way.

I remember I went to the party dressed all wrong and I ended up feeling like a teenager who tries to dress up as a gangster with things he's just found in a secondhand shop—the whole situation made me feel like I hadn't been paying attention to myself properly until then, as if all the details I'd been studying were completely irrelevant.

It was around this time that I began to feel that I'd lost the set of motivations with which I'd entered the situation (and country). Thus my position seemed useless and I found myself in Milan without any good reason.

One Saturday afternoon, soon after the Venice party, he invites me to his place for a beer. It is the first time I've been to his house, though we've half-known each other for a while. Until then, we had merely acknowledged each other's similarities from a distance, two people on secret missions in a city that permitted that way of living, in worlds that no one was sure actually existed.

First he shows me around the flat. It's on the top floor of the building, and we go to the balcony. He says:

"Listen, complete silence." He pauses to let me take it in. "You can never hear anything from here, it seems like you're out in the countryside."

Everything inside the apartment is at the height of better taste than other parochial Milanese fuckwits—at first this seems to be the general idea of its decoration. The guiding principle is profane, nasty, and funny. Custom-made furniture, a built-in bookshelf with a heavy industrial look, an iconic 90s sofa reupholstered in navy-blue wool with a beautiful Mexican blanket thrown over it, two or three small paintings from the early period of an artist who has recently become extremely famous.

I go up to his kitchen to look around and even the salt and pepper grinders are the Sottsass ones in different shades of coloured wood, one of his most gratingly nostalgic designs, exuding the most banal and straightforward spirituality. The only people who buy them are people who can't think of better status-symbol salt and peppershakers—"we can't have the Peugeots—so boring." They confirm my first suspicions of him: "Nicola is a fucking coward."

"And why shouldn't he be?" I find myself saying, immediately after, in the same breath.

I walk back down to the dining room without saying anything. I'm very happy to be there. I start looking at the books on his shelf, though he says most of them aren't his but his wife's.

He goes up to the kitchen to get us some beers and brings them back down to the table. He opens them and pours me a glass. It's a strange, sweetly flavored strong beer made from chestnuts. Later I find out it's produced by a relative of his but at the time it seems like a strange thing for him to have in the fridge.

We talk fairly casually to begin with.

He asks a few questions about the Giro d'Italia, playing on the television to our left, and about the sport in general, a sport in which I'm ostensibly an expert. I tell him about the dollar amounts behind a certain sponsorship, another rider's dissatisfaction with his equipment, the course this year, the stages where riders could take time, the general shift in tactics for these kinds of races over the last five years. He nods knowingly even though at moments my answers become very detailed, peppered with behind-the-scenes overheard conversations and insider politics. He nods knowingly, says "*si si*," and smiles.

I change the subject and try to talk a little about some of the things lying about that catch the eye: CDs, books, something that might prompt him to tell me some story about himself. But he remains vague, in a casual way, as though he wants to give the impression that he's forgetful, imprecise. It's a vagueness other people would read as part of his character and accordingly let it slide. I too let it slide, but I note the deliberateness of his actions.

I tell him I like a vase he has on the dining table, by a famous designer.

"The piece would have cost a lot, an investment," I say to him, inquiringly.

"Ahhh," he replies, "Yes maybe it's not even real, look underneath, no mark, no seal—hah hah—I got it from a friend who traffics in these things, yeah I'm not sure if it's real, it doesn't matter, right? Hah hah."

His objects don't seem like they are in the apartment directly, they don't seem personal so much as part of a plot, a long-running masquerade, a description of something in the form of severely compacted metaphor.

Things appear as signs, they exist in a descriptive capacity.

Quite excited suddenly, I look at him and recognize that he thinks you have to disguise the art you make. He thinks it should never arrive at explicit expression because the stakes are too unbearably low anywhere but in making it happen.

I want to tell him, here in the quiet of his apartment, that I recognize this in him. But as I try to begin, in tone more than words, he pretends not to know what I'm talking about, all the while looking at me with the most understanding eyes. His eyes alone seem to be proof of the existence of this secret world of making which we could share. But he refuses to vocally indulge me. I don't know what to do.

What follow are silences while I, bewildered, have to quite literally stop and rethink how to approach the situation. I can't think of what to ask him, how to make it clear that I want to discuss these things with him.

I ask him new sets of questions, so stark and artificial sounding as they break the silence that I stutter trying to articulate certain words clearly, struggling to get my tongue over the changes from vowels to consonants.

I try, searching for common ground, to talk to him directly about the city, the place I can barely believe we met each other in. I ask him, since I remember him telling me once that he'd lived abroad:

"Why the hell did you come back here, what for? What's this place got for you?"

"I have not come back," he says, "but I like it here, it's okay, I have my things that I like to do."

He goes on to make a snide remark about someone he went to lunch with recently who wants to leave but can't, "perfect targets—those kinds of Milanese," he says.

In response I make a noise that is supposed to sound like an insider's laugh.

I feel uneasy. It crosses my mind that I may be stuck in this city, that it's played some kind of trick on me. I ask him again, more pointedly, why he's here.

"But, I mean, what's the challenge? Why this city? Why didn't you make a clean break when you could?"

He admits, in response, to some banal longing, so distant from the grand network of subterfuge he has put in action in Milan.

"Sometimes I think I don't give a fuck, I wonder when I'm going to just go live in Mexico and write all day," he says.

It seems laughable to me as I look around him, at the objects peppering his flat.

It's clear, after that afternoon in his flat, our first proper meeting, that he doesn't want me as a friend. From what he says it is clear that any new friends would be completely super-fluous to his needs.

I decide I have to change my tack if I want to stay close to him. I don't want him to confess himself to me anyway, I think.

When I first met him he reminded me of something that had happened in another city. It was like a part of my past catching up with me and it made me secretly sick with fear.

It had been at a bar near the canals. He'd looked uglier to me then, more Italian, part of the same club of rich Italian boys everyone I met seemed to belong to. He looked like he had too much saliva in his mouth because his parents had overfed him, he had oddly heavy breath, you could smell it when he talked and it made me think he might stink of shit if you took his trousers off. I'd been introduced to him as he leaned at the bar, observing the crowd, paying for the drinks of a large group seated at a table but not joining them.

We immediately recognized—I made a joke about my jacket, implying a sort of expertise and he one-upped me; we both reached for the same word when describing the pleasures of the business we were in—that we had something in common, a kind of ability to move in and out of geographies, exploiting a sense of place, easily running along other people's consciousnesses—I acknowledged this similarity eagerly, he with a sort of laconic surprise.

He told me he'd lived in Los Angeles not so long ago.

He spoke to me calmly, as if from a great disinterested distance, but at the same time there was no doubt he was showing off.

It was the lies he told that reminded me of that past of mine that I hadn't encountered in a while. He was telling me the kinds of lies where the teller implies that things that have only happened to him once are long-running habits. Things about too much whiskey, Celine and De Sade, eating alone in expensive Japanese restaurants, knowing nobody (this last fact he would continue to repeat in later meetings, it seeming more barbarously unreal each time).

I said to myself automatically, "he's dangerous," thinking about the times in the past I'd told or listened to these lies, and the terrified evenings they'd always eventually led to, me shuddering alone, thinking, horrified "I'll never be anything but myself."

But for some reason after that afternoon in his flat I felt like those terms I'd been using were outdated, that they belonged to another city, that I needn't stay away, that this time it was going to be different.

What I feel is left to me, then, in the absence of a possibility for friendship, is a sort of parallelism, a closeness where he can't feel me touch him. A way of engaging with him without asking anything of him.

I try to familiarize myself with his decision-making process, to get comfortable with his intuitions. I try to follow them through an argument I overhear, a conversation we share, I try to find situations similar to his and superficially behave the same way I observed him behaving. And to do it all over and over again looking for patterns. And in so doing, I find I can become expert in things I know nothing of—the classic hustle (the hustler going round in circles), one that Nicola already knew.

He invites me around to his place quite frequently for a period after my first visit. Since I already know that he doesn't want me to be his friend I'm constantly wondering what it is he wants from me, why he wants to have me around him.

Each time he cooks for me it's ostensibly the style of food you cook if you don't give a fuck about cooking and entertaining for others, the kind of food you make if you only ever go shopping for yourself, with that kind of mindset, and that it wouldn't ever occur to you to do so any differently. The kind of thing you cook in a frying pan with a little bit of oil, starting with one small clove of garlic finely chopped, then adding from there, working from one smell released by the oil you like to another, enjoying yourself selfishly, nostrils over the pan. He makes a big show of cooking this way for other people.

One evening he invites me and someone else over and says he has nothing left in the house, that it will just be a plate of simple pasta. His kitchen has been designed like a turret, above the dining room, with a small opening from which he can look down and see what his guests do while they wait for the food to be prepared. We sit around, waiting, looking at the flat, shouting up to Nicola occasionally. I look at his custom-built cabinets, I remember the designer, a Greek who Nicola "discovered," telling me they'd gone to the supplier who manufactured the chipboard to choose the particular blue-green together. There are some Bjarne Melgaard drawings I hadn't noticed before artfully hung on the wall beneath the kitchen with two large paper clips.

Again I'm struck by how hard it is to believe he actually likes anything in here other than in a way that has nothing to do with him, in a kind of subterfuge that leaves him remote from the surface.

Again he says he has nothing in the house as he brings down the food, then tells me, as he sits down and puts some on my plate, first:

"You won't find a plate of pasta this good even at Noma."

The pasta is spaghetti cooked confidently al dente to the point that they seem very formal, intensely aware of their own consistency. The sauce is a simple, good quality passata with butter and mint. He asks me how good I think it is and I say very good (it is) but ask him what's in it.

"Passata with butter and mint?" I ask.

He shakes his head laughing, he raises his eyebrows like the kind of person who would eat shit while smiling at you daringly, making you feel like a fool for not doing likewise—

he shakes his head and refuses to go into detail. I ask again if it's just passata with butter and mint, and he says:

"I modified the ingredients. It was just what I had, it was a fantasy dish. I like to cook experimentally."

He uses an extremely technical Italian to describe how he balances the different properties of flavors.

Then he says to me:

"At times I've cooked the most delicious sauces on earth from a combination of what was left at home then immediately completely forgotten how I did them."

I imagine him conducting impromptu early morning dinner parties attended by men in space-age tuxedos, with an ominous sort of hygiene about them, glimmering eyes, hair-styles like designs for futurist world-land-speed-record automobiles and he, Nicola, dishing out, one at a time from his turret, plates of pasta with scientific sauces made from the same single-person shopping resources to the acclaim of the men below who applaud crisply each time a plate is served. Pasta with dried apricots, garlic and capers, pasta with anchovies, cream, olives, lemon and chocolate… I have the thought a little too quickly and it unnerves me, I stammer a little when I ask for more pasta, a gesture I had intended to use to demonstrate an informality and ease with the company.

When he clears the plates (I don't offer to help—as though even that level of collaboration might be distasteful to him), I go to the bathroom, before I open the door he says down from the kitchen, "That one doesn't work—go downstairs, there's another down there."

I've never been downstairs before, the first few times he showed me round he declined to even mention that such a part of the flat existed. I walk down the new-ish cast iron staircase he's had installed. Below there is one medium-sized room with a double bed in the middle and a bathroom attached to the far corner. The bedroom is dark. The two small windows are covered with curtains. The sheets on the bed are a dark grey or blue. To the left of the bed are bookshelves made in the same style as those on the floor above. Even though the ceilings are considerably lower down here, these bookshelves seem more ominous, probably because of their proximity to the bed; they seem to lean over where Nicola and his wife sleep. On this bookshelf, I notice, there are fewer books, more messily arranged, some fallen, some straight, some with their front covers facing out so as to be visible from the bed, some at rough angles as if they'd been thrown back. There are also piles and piles of magazines, mostly fashion and music, at the base, in front of the bookshelf not in it. The magazines date back at least ten years and seem well-thumbed. Some sit casually in a way that suggests they were once even adored, treated by their reader like entire worlds. I look at the titles on the shelf without rushing. It will seem natural to Nicola, I think, for me to have been interested.

I notice there are also what seem to be posters underneath the bed, rolled up pieces of paper, tubes, barely visible. I get on my knees and reach underneath, searching for I don't know what, keeping my eye on the staircase. Beneath the tubes I feel loose sheets of large wrinkled paper. But the wrinkles, I notice with my hands, are ordered, structured, expert. They are pieces of paper meant to be folded, I guess, to a smaller size. Using the tips of my fingers, I pull back a few loose sheets, growing a little nervous about what I'm doing, thinking I might be going a little too far.

I pull the sheets out from under the bed and look. The sheets are dusty, they've probably been there at least a year.

"Maps."

I look at them quickly. He has annotated them, there are a few arrows linking the words, the words all seem important, earnest. The way they've been arranged makes them look like notes for a novel.

I push them back under the bed and go to the bathroom and piss as quickly as possible before going back upstairs where I make a few considered but jokey remarks about the books and magazines he reads. He just smiles.

After dinner we drink some whiskey from a bottle with an oddly minimal white and aqua-green label; after pouring a second glass we move out onto the balcony, sit down at the table and talk there.

He looks at his watch. He makes a comment about what he's going to do tomorrow. I ask him if I'm disturbing, if I should leave.

"I like to wake up early," he says.

"Yeah, me too, how early?"

"Four, five."

"Still dark?"

"Uh-huh."

"What for?"

"To work. To write."

I don't turn around to look at it but I imagine him at his desk, with low sloping ceiling directly above and its view of the balcony in front, him serious, composed, ambitious, writing decisively, taking pleasure in it.

"Woah. And you don't get tired?"

"I like to go back to sleep afterwards. That's the best, around ten or eleven."

Silence follows. Then we begin talking about business again, opportunities, ideas, clothing brands from the city. We are drunker and more enthusiastic, both smiling.

Later on, in a moment after a pause in the conversation I think I hear him ask me, abruptly and explicitly (with his absolutely remote decisiveness) if I need him to do me "any favours," or something along those lines. There seems to be a moment of completely open exchange between us, the two writers, clear and transparent, just me and him in the empty city. I don't know how to respond, everything inside me stumbles at the point of articulation leaving me dumb, feeling surprisingly empty, and the moment passes.

4

I wake up early in the morning, before the alarm I'd set a few hours ago when we got into the hotel goes off.

The shutters are drawn—not the way I usually sleep—all the windows are closed and all you can smell in the room is the mixed stagnant breaths of Nicola and I, sitting low and heavy. The sheets on the bed aren't even pulled out properly, I slept like a mummy, my feet encased tightly at the bottom in order not to appear too comfortable.

He, in fact, seems to have slept anonymously, like a neutral object, another piece of the room's uninteresting furniture, he has made very little of the bed, his hands have not grasped at any part of it, there exists no familiarity between him and the sheets or pillow, barely even an acknowledgement.

I'm still heavy with the alcohol of the night before, moving heavily, I get out of the bed and put my jeans and shoes on, pick up my jacket, I don't even go to take a piss, I'm just about to leave when I hear him say to me,

"You're leaving now?"

I'd wanted to leave before he awoke, without a noise, to prove a point. His voice, then, almost makes me jump.

"Yeah yeah yeah… I have to go… back up to Milan, to interview… that guy, for the book. Thanks… thanks so much for letting me sleep in your room last night, and getting me into the party, everything thanks."

"*Figurati*," he says. As if he'd known all along I was going to ask to stay the night there and he truly didn't care, found it irrelevant, neither pleasant nor unpleasant.

I leave the room and go out into the corridor. The light is extremely strong, the walls are painted mint green and white, I still don't understand what the natural light of the day is, if outside it will be light or dark, sunny or overcast. I bump the hallway with my shoulders, I can't walk straight down through it.

I manage to get into the lift, which is tiny, full of mirrors and still too much light, and take it down to the ground floor. There I see the natural light directly for the first time that morning as it shines in from the large entrance doors. The delightful anxiety of my rush out of the room ends and slowly the tone of my vision adjusts. From the large reception area, whose luxurious ornamentation seems a little brusque, un-enamored with the labor of its details (and thus scrubbed of its past), I go to the desk and speak with the large genial-looking man behind the counter. Unable to stop thinking about my heavy breath I try to speak with as little wind as possible, to just release my words rather than push them out, looking down a bit, so that the smells of my mouth might not come out. I ask him where the train station is and how long it takes to get there.

I listen to his instructions, thank him and leave walking extremely quickly. While walking I try to think what the perfect breakfast would be at this point.

"Just a coke?" I ask myself.

"A brioche?"

"Coffee and brioche?"

"Imagine being able to get something fried …"

"McDonalds at the station?"

When I do actually get to the station I buy a coke and my ticket and get straight on a train for Milan. I sit back in the seat and the night's memories begin releasing their heat.

How do you act around somebody who seems to know everything? Where do you stake your ground?

The previous afternoon we'd driven down out of Milan to go to this party together. Ostensibly it was an important work occasion for him, and I, through one connection or other, after hearing he was attending, had been able to make it seem natural enough that I too might be required down there.

We arrived together but at the moment when we entered the space of the party he appeared, even to me who knew better, to have arrived alone, as if gliding out from behind black stage curtains.

He immediately hung back as I walked in, went quietly towards a corner and from there began moving back towards the centre, in a different, looser fashion, with his eyes feigning a sort of absent mindedness, scanning the room softly in smooth arcs, without any apparent need to settle on anything.

He moved through the party making himself known in an indistinct accumulative way, one nod after the other, one quiet word and touch of hands where necessary. It was as though he didn't really need to be there, as though his presence was casual and fortuitous.

It was as though nobody should know where he actually did the things that mattered to him. Where he organized his thoughts had to remain his most obscured element.

After a few minutes we found each other again and walked to the bar together. I offered to pay for the beers and he said:

"Look," opening his wallet, indicating to it with his eyes, "I only came out with €10, I'll pay for the first round then I've got nothing left, okay?"

I realized that the evening was going to end up costing me more than if I'd caught the train down. I nodded.

It was the most normal trick in the hustler's book, the one an old hand might like to pull every now and then just to show he still had it the same way he had it when he was a teenager, getting himself drunk on other people's money all night.

I wasn't angry about the humiliation, being treated like a mark. I felt a serene nothingness as I imagined all the money in my wallet being spent. It felt as though the bills in it had become faceless. I couldn't say anything in response. Later, I was secretly glad for the long corridor his gesture opened up onto his younger self, his childish ambition. I imagined him years earlier coming into the city, with a sort of spoilt expectation of what being smarter than everyone else meant he deserved.

He walked off with his drink and I observed him for a while as I made extremely small talk with a colleague of his.

That night his actions seemed to be performed as if by remote control. He exercised his power the way a bomb maker does; the results of his decisions were inflicted without his visible participation.

Everything he wanted to make happen seemed prepared well before he arrived.

And when these things happened he was there, on the pavement in front of the building apparently ignoring what had happened (though a miniscule delay in his breath revealed otherwise), seeming disinterested, or casual, or posing for the event's official photographer with all the time in the world, making a really big deal, through a certain strange permanence in his eyes, of how little his body moved towards what it apparently belonged to, how it was only sliding where you expected it to slide, making the lie or truth that came most easily, that mostly easily accommodated your question.

He looked loose, and his clothes were exactly how I imagined they appeared when he laid them out on the bed before putting them on, with all the same arbitrary crumples and objectivity.

Did he realize how good-looking he'd become?

A little later he came over to me and said he was going to the dinner and that I should come.

"But I'm not invited," I objected.

"*Gatecrash dude*," he said leeringly, switching into English, before breaking out into a soft laugh.

"Okay, okay," I said. Around him, strangely, I didn't feel afraid of anything. I couldn't imagine anything going wrong, there seemed to be no point in thinking I was still shackled to who I feared I really was.

We began to walk towards the restaurant, one of the city's two finest, all together in a big group. I chatted comfortably with a few of the overseas guests I knew, trying to prepare as familiar an attitude as possible as I got ready to enter the restaurant and find an empty place.

Nicola walked up to me near the entrance, then slid a little to the side and I followed him.

"Just sit down somewhere empty," he said, "seating is assigned, I don't know if there is a place for you, I didn't ask the guy who's organizing the dinner. Maybe you will get lucky, *gatecrasher*."

"Okay, it shouldn't be a problem," I said, really believing it. I waited for a few people to pass then walked in. The overseas guests were at the table of honor, the guests would have been too carefully selected there, so I moved along. The only other person I knew there was Nicola. I walked around a little more and then headed to his table.

"Is there anybody there? I think that's my seat," I asked him indicating the seat next to him.

"No, there's nobody sitting here. *Accomodati.*"

And nobody came over and humiliated me out of my seat. In fact from the moment I sat down, I ceased to even consider the possibility and instead looked forward to the food.

After the main course had been served, the dinner slowly dragged on, desserts started coming out, some coffee, people got up and mixed, exchanged seats.

Right beneath the restaurant, which looked out onto a park, there was a club of some kind, full of kids it seemed, when I leant over the edge to have a look. The entire building that housed the club and restaurant was made from white stucco. Lots of arches instead of doors. Down below the kids were drifting in and out of the covered, darker part of the club where the DJ was playing.

Somebody at the table said maybe it was a school holiday tomorrow and that was why it was so packed below. Nicola got up, I looked at him, I found that he was already turning to look at me; he nodded his head in the direction of the stairs and said, "Shall we go have a look?"

I got up and followed him. We walked around the perimeter of the building towards the club, we went through an open-air part leading to the entrance, our heads swiveling quickly like rogue security cameras, staring at everyone, taking in information. Before we crossed the threshold he turned and smiled as if to say that it was him showing me all this.

We headed towards the front, where we saw a thick-bodied man with long straightened dyed hair dressed in women's flared jeans, enormous black shiny sneakers and a lace tank top dancing on top of a very small mock-stage, a coffee-table basically used as an improvised method for highlighting the spectacle. The music was a snarling, crunching hip-hop. People were standing around watching, some filming it on their phones, there was also a professional photographer. I stood next to the photographer, with nobody between us and the performer. The dancer tried to get other people to dance with him, people backed away a little, one enthusiastic girl came out and moved around the dancer, a little unsure, trying to get into the flow.

Suddenly I realized that I was grimacing, pushing my eyebrows together, crossing my arms sternly.

I turned and looked at Nicola who was about fifteen feet away, to the left. He had his back to a pylon, bending his knees strangely and tentatively in rhythm with the sound. His arms were by his sides, loosely, in a way that was impossible to imitate. (I tried it then and my arms felt like they were going to float off my body so I crossed them again.) I looked at his face. He was smiling slightly. I couldn't tell what year of his life the look came from.

A familiar panic fluttered across my stomach but I knew I would have to keep it together a little longer yet.

Then he turned and saw me looking at him. Though he wasn't surprised, I thought I detected the subtle annoyance of having something confirmed for him. He started walking back out. I got in behind him, following him. When we got out he turned to me a little and I came up to his side.

When we got back upstairs waiters were still bringing out platters of espressos. I took one and moved out to the large balcony. There was a tall Scandinavian looking out at the park. He turned and said hello. He was dressed in the usual tastefully up-to-date fairly expensive clothes people like him always wear.

He told me he was an architect. He told me he'd just been up in Milan for work and then stayed on a day to come down to this dinner, to see the person who organized it, "an old friend," he said pompously, even though he was no older than thirty and the host was in his early sixties.

I vaguely elaborated a reason why I was there, creating an approximate thread of potential friends and collaborators that might exist between us.

He started talking about "Miuccia."

"Miuccia is lovely, yes. She is really brilliant, there are very few people like her, maybe a genius. I think she is the best in fashion, definitely the number one in Milan."

"Really? Yeah she does seem pretty special, I always have liked her stuff, a great strange understanding of perverse Italian glamour, teenage, repressed or something very funny like that. She must be wickedly funny to hang around with."

"Yes and you know nobody says it but her company is the best organized in the whole of the Milan fashion industry, she's really professional, and Patrizio does a great job helping her with that side of things. I love working with Miuccia, for me it's always a pleasure dealing with her, I was here this week for her actually."

"Uh huh."

I saw Nicola at the other side of balcony and moved over towards him. I said,

"Do you know that guy?" Gesturing with my eyes towards the Scandinavian.

"No, who is he?"

"Hah hah he was just telling me about what good friends he is with Miuccia."

"Yeah, then what the fuck is he still doing here tonight, eh?"

Back in Milan that morning after the train ride, I feel ready for an enormous load of work, a load that won't eventuate that day. I feel strong, my limbs tough and tensed like industrial springs.

I don't have anything much to do.

So I walk around the city looking for something to do. I walk on the bridge over Porta Garibaldi station, down past Corso Como and through Brera. Near the Accademia my phone rings.

It's a friend from London.

"Where are you?" he asks quickly. I tell him.

He says to me to straight away, "I've just come from an appointment."

"Uh-huhh," I say slowly.

"You know, with," he tries to be serious, "a mistress."

"Uh-huhhhh."

"Now I've got some time to kill actually," he says, still seriously, "you know, between appointments."

"Yesss—what's the next appointment?"

He tells me he's got an appointment up in North London, with a man, an Arab man or an Italian man he's not sure, but this guy is going to suck him off for free as long as he doesn't say anything. He has six hours, he tells me, until the next appointment. I can hear the sounds of the road coming through from the phone, I realize he's out walking as well.

He wants to know what to do between appointments, he's calling to ask for suggestions.

Suddenly I'm very excited. I imagine him walking the streets. I wish I were there, gliding between these kinds of sexual encounters, which are linked together for him only by their type of availability.

We joke a bit about it, I tell him he should dive down into some bar and get on the stage and perform, tell a stream of pathetic jokes, then leave before the audience has time to respond. Keep moving.

He giggles and we end the conversation shortly after.

I keep walking, the city completely resistant.

At the lights I see a man crossing briskly with a black leather briefcase in hand. He is wearing a light grey suit with four buttons and high lapels, a white shirt and navy blue tie—all in all a fairly traditional outfit for Milanese businessmen of the area. Then I look up to his face and see that he is wearing a pair of white, red and yellow sports sunglasses. It's a compelling look, I don't understand it, I look closer to see what the sunglasses are exactly—"Carrera"—but they must be originals I think—not reissues. Or are they a reissue? I'm not sure.

I look at him again, with his ridiculous sunglasses.

A photo of him would convince most outsiders of the quotidian stylishness and sophistication of the city—it would confirm some idea of Milan which has international currency. I wonder if he is secretly having a good laugh about this. He seems terrifically ignorant of what people outside his small social circle would think of him, his posture is stiffly vain.

I imagine the story behind his sunglasses. They're not reissues, they're some element from his past, he has decided to start wearing them again because Carrera is reissuing that exact model, or he has noted that other companies are performing similar vintage reissue operations and he thinks it's funny. Maybe. He remembers he has these old sunglasses that might be so very vogue-ish now. He finds them amongst his old ski jackets in his basement, exactly where he remembered having left them after a holiday in '92. Something along these lines. Whatever humor or irony is present in his wearing the sunglasses is entirely private, they relate to some story of his, not some broader social phenomena. He doesn't feel the pressure of fashion when he sees the reissue or similar styled glasses being issued by other brands, he just sees a memory awakened, a private story of his own life continued.

The motivations for aesthetic decisions are a layering of histories, of stories, they are not brand new superficial looks disconnected from their heritage ravaging the youths of a city—no—they are an accumulation in time, of times, like you'd never expect to see in a supposedly big city. No—here on the surface of the city you still see things that happened previously more clearly than anywhere else, even if nobody cares to share their meaning with you.

I continue moving with this kind of fervor in my thoughts. I run into someone I half-know, I explain that the walk is unaccountable, that it started small and now I have to keep going, I have created a series of reasons to progress, dotting the map with places to visit. I am trying through perseverance to make something happen.

I continue on without much luck but that elastic tension in my muscles doesn't die, my attention to it dulls, certainly, but it remains there, now without the surprise which accompanied it that morning.

I end up in a bar on the canals, the same one where I first met Nicola. I go there for the promise of an international crowd. People who question you aggressively about your accent from a paranoia that someone might have found them out—people who left London or some other capital for reasons best not disclosed, some professional humiliation they are too vain to even admit to themselves let alone make light of here, thousands of kilometers away. But that day my eye can't catch anything except maybe the celery stalks seemingly sprouting from the sink behind the bar, attended to occasionally by the bartender when someone orders a Bloody Mary. I'm standing at the bar deliberating. I want to get so drunk I can no longer see. But as my eyes scan the options I'm raving at myself, angry at the delicacy of my body, the way it responds to these stimuli I want to give it. "It's all poison." Something inside me is insisting. "Alcohol is poison. Behind my neck. Cheap spirits with too much sugar. Pinching the muscles of my neck. Making them ache unbearably sharply. It's all poison. Alcohol, white flour, white sugar, to only eat food which has no effect on the body, the bread, and water of this world."

By this point a guy I half-know is standing at the bar talking to me. He's wearing an assortment of vague, fluttering status symbols, which I barely recognize anyway, or little more than I do his goatee; expensively crumpled linens and cottons in shades of brown and grey, nothing that sticks—a real waste of money, I'm thinking—"Yeah I went to the party last Thursday," the guy is saying, referring to a particularly raunchy private party we'd both been invited to during a week when I was away, "I left early, yeah I went, but I know that I'm interested in other things, let's put it like that."

"I know I'm interested in other things?" The phrase sticks in my head. I don't hang around long and go home, not out of fatigue, or if it is fatigue it's a fatigue that has to do with boredom and little else.

"Interested in other things"? To live according to what you know you're interested in? It seems laughable to me, as I think of it back in my small flat, posturing with exaggerated ease at the chair in front of my desk, playing with my haircut, pushing it up, to one side, to the other, patting it to try to deduce what kind of shape its taken, walking to the mirror and back in different shirts I've bought since moving here, wondering if I look more or less Italian.

The next night I'm out at the same bar again, though. If someone had asked me why right there on the spot I wouldn't have had a good reason. I would have had a reason, a bland one, one invented for the potential pleasure of others: "I've heard the crowd here is international," I might have joked (again), or if someone from overseas were visiting I would have told them sardonically, "I've been here long enough now that if I go there I always run into someone I know"—laughing again, this time with pathetic insistence.

But in fact when I go down there I do run into someone I know. A guy called Gianluca, a friend of Nicola's. I see him before he sees me, he is greeting somebody who probably barely knows him with a complete excess of familiarity and intimacy. The way he works the bar makes him look desperate on so many different levels. Like a brilliant actor (looking at him I wish Italy had some kind of grungy macho indie film-maker to make him an icon before he turns thirty and loses his chance, but it doesn't and I can just imagine him sliding into a more and more desperate, grasping patheticism as he grows older), for every part he plays, every bluff he pulls, he always manages to reveal the hidden motive to the audience—a brilliant actor who doesn't realize he's an actor.

He comes and greets me, also in an excessively familiar manner but because I understand him I think I deserve it. I tell him, in response to his greeting:

"Gianluca you should be an actor."

He ignores this.

He asks me a few questions about where I've been, when I got back, and I give vague answers, not really interested in being familiar to him in that way.

He asks about Nicola, our chief friend in common and the person who introduced us. Gianluca adores Nicola, is terrified of him. He doesn't tell me this, in fact he acts like a person who doesn't ever even think about Nicola, who is friends with him through some natural coincidence, perhaps some natural sym-pathy, but of course being the exquisite actor that he is, his pauses, the brief flickers of calculation between his responses to surprising questions, reveal clearly and intelligently that thoughts of Nicola keep him up every night in confusion, guessing at Nicola's motives in the dark, unable to understand how long their supposed friendship will last and what qualities Nicola finds attractive in him. But since he does not know he is an actor he might not even know he has these thoughts, he might think that what he thinks about at night when he can't sleep is how he can emulate Nicola, how he can operate in the same privileged sphere of power, contacts, and action as Nicola's.

Actually the way he works the room is a distinct imitation of Nicola. When we finish exchanging the three or four updates we can share with each other about our overlapping lives he pretends to see someone over my shoulder that he absolutely must speak to and leaves me at the bar.

I don't bother finding someone else to speak to in his absence. I watch him do his Nicola imitation. Even though it's hot inside, full of people, Gianluca is wearing an oversized military jacket with the collar up. He has a thick beard and is wearing a baseball cap pulled low over his eyes. He is extremely thin and a little short.

He tries to do two things at once in his imitation: he tries to look like he has no investment in anything that is happening and at the same time that he knows exactly what is happening, to himself particularly, at any one given moment.

Someone speaks to him and he doesn't look at them while they speak, he makes his eyes glaze over a little as he looks up to his left eyes still glazed, puts a toothpick in his mouth with his left hand. Then, as the guy gets close to finishing what he's saying Gianluca's eyes unglaze. He removes the toothpick and his expression changes to mild irritation. Then finally he turns to the person who's speaking, wipes the irritation off his face, opens his eyes a little wider, showing all their brown color and nods extremely seriously.

Like watching a good movie where about thirty minutes in, in a moment when the two protagonists express, in a frank exchange, their characters' defining motives that will allow the story to continue, for one to share his or her strange life with the other, but the motive is incorrect, psychologically wrong, unrealistic, laughably ignorant of interior currents running through the story up until that point—just like that, at some point Gianluca's imitation fills me with frustration. I stand there thinking angrily, ready to jump into action though I can't think of any specific action to jump into—he's so stupid that in his imitation he reveals to me his pathetic, childish, and undeveloped motives, not Nicola's opaque ones, not the quality that keeps Nicola afloat no matter where he goes, so tensely balanced in the action.

I turn away and try to find someone else I half-know to speak with.

"Nobody here understands anything," I think. "Nicola can get away with murder."

Later just as Gianluca is leaving, Nicola arrives alone, and they intersect at the threshold of the bar, like a spinning revolving door—caught in the motion of being launched out of it, Gianluca recognizes Nicola and tries momentarily to stop the imaginary door, his face saying nothing but his upper body stiffening, revealing the adrenaline shot he has just received.

Nicola arrives alone but is meeting someone there, a girl who is just visiting briefly. She is already in a circle of friends who are glad to see her again and Nicola edges towards the circle with a martini, his shoulders turned slightly inwards, to make himself small. He tabs himself onto the group at an angle, on the woman's left side. When his shoulder touches her as he edges into the group, she turns and steps back so they can begin talking.

She is not particularly good looking, she is tall and pleasant, she must be exactly the same age as him, but unlike him she's not at all ambiguous about this, if she looks a little weary it is with happy autonomy—her intelligence, clear in the time she allows herself to respond to what is happening, seems relatively absent of vanity.

From the way she looks at him it seems that he probably loved her, with unreserved adulation, when they were younger—a love based on conversation, exchange of ideas. He, on the other hand, tries to encourage her to put her desires on him, rocking gently on the back of his feet, listening to her with nuanced openness, passive and accommodating. I see that in certain moments he, strangely, forgets this role and begins searching her face expectantly, more boyishly than I've ever seen him previously, as if all he's waiting to see is if she will let him fuck her again in a few hours.

The bar is at almost full capacity now. My choice of drinks starts getting heavier. I buy one for Nicola and I'm quite drunk when I leave so he must have also bought me at least one at some point though I can't remember.

To write about another writer in the city, to write parallel to him, sidle up to him, keep it your secret, yearn for him silently every time you see him. To constantly observe him, and then to forget why you started doing so in the first place. To walk around the empty city together. To want to give everything to a person to whom you can't show the things you consider most important.

This is what has happened to me with Nicola, this is the position I find myself in, I realize, as we walk back to his house, accompanying him there after the bar closes. I'm not sure what exact excuse I give for accompanying him to the gate of his building, whether it's that there is a bus I can get from down there or a bar just down the road to the left where I think I might have some friends waiting for me. Either way he certainly knows I'm lying, but he obliges.

We walk back, side by side, talking drunkenly about what I (but not him) could have done differently back at the bar with the girls I was speaking to. He is gently and intelligently chiding me with a delicate boredom, a kind frustration. He uses the word "pussy" so much I imagine it must be becoming a metaphor for what he feels about something else entirely. He is quite drunk but that doesn't change the way I feel I can act, I'm still just as nervous and unable to assume that there is any warmth between us, he seems ready to go off and do his own thing at any moment, even as we stand in front of the gate of his building and he says he is going up. I look at his bare neck with a bit of stubble on it—the city is quiet, there are just a few people walking down the street and the sound of a tram, his trousers are baggy and I imagine his balls and dick loose and pendulous within the trousers, dry and fresh. What's it like to really "go home" with Nicola?

I go home, not with him but back to my flat. I open the balcony doors, the only way to let light into the place even though at this hour there is no light, just the noise of weak motorbikes dragging themselves up the road just to the right of the courtyard my flat faces. They look so good, the doors, pinned back to the wall, as open as possible. The recently mopped tiles of my floor shine cleanly. I switch on the small light next to my desk, take off my shoes, socks, and jeans and sit down in my briefs and t-shirt. I look outside, a few neighbors' lights are still on but I can't hear them, I can feel a cool breeze slowly creep in and touch my bare legs, my toes. I look at the chipped cement on the floor of the balcony, and the little piles of squashed chalkstone, now white powder, which have fallen from the external walls. I turn my gaze away from outside and towards the computer. I don't feel so drunk even though I know I am because I feel the need to throw up every time I close my eyes and already can't remember anything about the actual time Nicola and I spent in the bar. But my mind seems to be working clearly and my thoughts fairly lucidly. I check some blogs to see if there have been any new posts. I go to a blog of a Milanese photographer, friend of Nicola's, nothing new, but I'm bored so I stay on the site this time, and just staring at it wondering what to do next when I notice the "random" button at the top of the page. I hit it—

a photo from 2006 of flowers. I hit it again—a photo of Beirut. Again—a photo from this year in Mexico City. And again—this time I find a photo of Nicola I've never seen before, it surprises me, it's a photo taken at night in a bar— my surprise is fearful as much as anything else—the night of the photo swims unreservedly with my own night, as though we are in the same place. In it he is standing against a wall with a small ledge for drinks (there are two beer bottles visible), dressed in his white suit. He is almost doubled over, he seems to be collapsing to the floor and next to him there is a man standing upright, with an enormous hat casting his face in shadows—underneath is written "Mexico City—2011." I open it in a new tab, getting it at its highest resolution and then save it, putting it into a folder of photos of him I've started collecting, to help me try to focus these thoughts that keep escaping me at the moment they're supposed to be realized into some kind of articulation.

5

He probably left the country like a criminal. Everyone knows how a criminal leaves. Even the blandest mainstream film regains precision when the criminal leaves. He can leave at will, and when he does, he leaves without anyone noticing. Hunted by enormous bodies of manpower, he slips quietly through the elaborate net cast to prevent his escape, thanks to his intimacy with the boroughs. Sliding on foot through car parks in grey industrial complexes without ever making a fuss, nodding to the police, even touching the peak of his baseball cap as he passes because he's just an ordinary man moving ordinarily to a harmless appointment. Working quietly, in miniscule fractions and margins of error, a matter of seconds between one train leaving and the next, the doors closing moments before a possible captor gets on, his eyes well and truly nailed to the back of his head; near misses hold no suspense, because the only thought he can ever conceive of is *nothing changes*. The train pushes and pulls as the carriages knock against each other before it finds equilibrium and slowly chugs out of there.

Online there are traces of this time he spent overseas, in China, in Los Angeles, and in Mexico City. There are mentions of his name dotting the map, a noted attendance at a conference in Shenzen, an interview at a trade show in Pasadena, a footnote in an academic paper claiming he was interviewed in Los Angeles, a credit for collaboration on a short film shot in Mexico City.

In the few photos from the period that are publicly available he seems extraordinarily thin—the kind of thinness you never get back once you lose it. His clothes may or may not be expensive, but they hang off him as if they were made of linens woven specifically for African climates. His face in these photos, apart from revealing that fast-burning skinniness, expresses a rare beauty, in fact it's this particular beauty that shakes the attentive viewer out of any other thought, slapping and forcing them to pay attention. His face is like a magnet pulling narratives across a landscape, showing a mass of complex stories of movement. It's a beauty that has nothing to do with the realm of physical attraction and everything to do with self-invented destinies.

In some photos, those where he's deliberately posing or that were taken during the evening, his face has an eager shine that can't last, like someone who drinks a beautiful rum cocktail thirstily, as though it were a soft drink.

These photos aren't precisely dated and the exact place where they were taken is unclear but they must coincide with some internal euphoria.

It's hard to be sure where he went first, Los Angeles or Mexico City, but either way he immediately found the heat different. It was the heat of insects scuttling underground, across the formica floor, buzzing around excrement or decomposing fruit, rather than the heat of humans. The heat, he would have noted, contained moisture that gave life to these things, allowing them to spread and multiply.

He was drawn to parts of the city that seemed to agree with him, that seemed to feel the same way, ghettos with proportions that allowed him to move according to patterns his mind was picking up in the atmosphere.

In these places, stores seemed to stay open all day and night, not because they were bleached twenty-four-hour consumer paradises but because the people in the store didn't have anywhere else to go to sleep, or to cook or drink or even socialize. Maybe that's why the sounds in those areas rarely seemed to rise above a murmur, as if everyone was tired because they never went to sleep or were being quiet because people were sleeping right next to them and they didn't want to disturb them.

He would have regularly frequented the bars in these areas, bars that did not even think to offer their patrons indoor seating. There were white or green plastic chairs and stools splayed in the front, and if you were lucky a tarpaulin in case of rain. The part of the bar counter where one could buy drinks was at the entrance, it was impossible to go further in, usually because all the interior space was used to stack crates of beer, or maybe sometimes cardboard boxes of salted snacks—the space inside, where the beer crates stood, and beyond, looked like a room to him, a normal room that could serve as a bar, but something made him unsure of his judgment, as if one were to remove all the beer crates and boxes the room would reveal itself to be something different and strange, something maybe he'd never seen before—something frightening, he imagined.

His phone calls home would have probably been made from these bars, towards the beginning of the evening, although he often stayed out late. They would have been made after a period of first conversing with himself.

These monologues were at first full of images of flying objects cutting through the air quickly, making a low whistling sound: he imagined an arrow rushing through a forest on an early morning, where the fog was just beginning to rise and the ground was covered in dew. He pictured himself as this quiet cutting edge of a steaming, recently awoken, place: the lonesome hero of his own life.

When he took his beer back to his seat at the plastic table he would watch the moisture outside the glass fall into a ring at the bottom; then he would put his phone next to the glass, close to the beads of moisture. The telephone was an enormous shiny black expensive thing he'd bought at the airport before leaving, imagining that something at once so vulgarly aspirational and businesslike would be the most innocuous accessory he could have around the low lifes he planned to keep company with.

He looked at the phone on the table next to the beer, and, as was more or less usual for those evenings, around the time the phone made its first appearance, he began the conversations with himself:

"Who knows I'm here now?" He asked this question first because the answer gave him pleasure:

"Nobody." "Nobody knows I'm here." "I must have disappeared." It was amazing for him to think it had happened so quickly, this vanishing. "No one knows where I am," he said again.

Time was different when you felt forgotten.

He looked at the phone.

"Who could I call? Who could I call out of the blue and surprise? Someone who has absolutely no idea even what country I'm in. To awake myself in them. Who could I call?"

And then he would make the calls, to people very far away who he imagined could appreciate the breathlessness he spoke with, the sudden bullet of emotions he felt compelled to inject into the conversation, the enormous amount of force he had to summon to invent himself as something entirely new for them. As he spoke, he felt like he was emerging from darkness, glistening and beautiful, and that the people listening to him on the other side loved him. They loved him uselessly, he realized after the calls, because he represented an impossible love, the one who without thinking much, during melancholy, indulgent evenings, they might call the one that "could have been."

When he spoke to them he would unwind enormous stories, almost all to do with evenings that hadn't ended. He'd begin, and this would even later become a joke he'd mock himself with, without even saying hello, or at least not waiting for so much as the confirmation that the person on the other side of the line could hear him:

"Hey—hey? Hey, ok, it's me. I'm here sitting in the bar with no inside area again."

"It's mostly white people here but across in the corner I can see about twelve guys and three girls, Africans, really dark skin, all sitting against the wall of a half-open shop, drinking beer and spirits, I can hear them speaking about four languages, nobody seems to speak all of them, it jumps back and forth, casually, dangling sometimes …"

Then:

"Last night I was out with some people I met at a bar, one further down from here, where the buildings are closer together, almost an alleyway. I was there talking on the phone for something to do with work and these people overheard me speaking Italian—you know how the provincial mindset works, girls whose idea of a more exciting boyfriend is somebody who is 'foreign or something like that,' anyway I heard a girl giggling behind me and some bits of what she was saying to the guys she was with and then all four of them, three guys and the girl, came a little closer to me and I turned around to look at them and smiled nice and big and said *hello*.

"The girl said she'd overheard me speaking Italian, she asked me where I was from. *Italy*, I said, then I laughed and then said *Milan*. She told me that she and her friends were going up to a party in the hills now if I wanted to come. She said they had space in the car and that I could come with them. I said sure.

"I didn't say much in the car, I was looking out the window as we started taking roads out of the city and up the hills. Every now and then it worried them that I was silent and they asked me if I was having a nice time. I said 'yeah, sure, of course,' and laughed again.

"The party they took me to first was in a really big house with good views, the guy whose party it was looked like some pseudo-hippy, an emotionally damaged rich boy, eyes always waiting for the pain to set in. You could see the city from up there, and hear it as well, distantly, I could hear music from a specific nightclub down there, really intense old techno.

"I wasn't talking too much there either, mostly walking around. Then I heard some noise, some violent shouting between a few people, one person sort of grunting in a low voice like a crazy being restrained, another person shouting back something that had to do with one guy being black or an immigrant, or something like that. I went around the corner to the side of the house where it was happening, I stood next to the guy who'd been shouting the racist stuff, and looked at the guy who was being restrained. They were trying to fight, there was a lot of scuffling, the guy who had been abused wouldn't shut up or calm down. The pseudo-hippy whose house it was came out. He looked at me as if I'd brought this supposedly racist guy in and said to me *we can't believe you'd ruin the delicate emotional ecosystem we've created here.* I didn't feel like correcting him.

"*Fuck you.*

"Then one of the guys who had invited me who must have been watching came up to me and said *why don't we go to another party?*—he was very calm, he didn't care much what anyone thought. So we all went out together, him and me and the girl and the other two guys.

"This other party was completely different, really quiet, like a drug party or an uncommonly sexy swinger's party. The people were high or drunk and sitting on the sofas together speaking quietly, mostly couples, or in the kitchen holding big red plastic cups of alcohol talking about films or poetry.

"I walked through the place and nobody seemed to notice me, definitely nobody acknowledged my presence, I looked at the structure of the house, where the exits were, which room led to another, how many bathrooms per bedroom. I walked into one bedroom and saw a girl half-sleeping while a guy touched her, it didn't look like either of them wanted to have sex, though, they both looked emotionally lazy. Then I went outside into the garden. I realized I had a cup in my hand with some good whiskey in it. I drank a bit of it. I could see another couple leaned up in the dirt against the fence with their hands under each other's waistbands.

"Once I finished the whiskey and couldn't smell its expensive perfume wafting up from the glass anymore I began to smell moisture in the air around me, mixing with the grass and dirt of the garden. I realized I was actually really cold and that the moisture was forming on my t-shirt as well, my nipples were hard.

"I stood there and looked around me, at the hills and the city below.

"I had these images in my head of my knees buckling and me just collapsing to the floor like a sack of potatoes. I tried to half do it there in the garden, I let my knees half go, I started falling, then I straightened and stiffened again.

"Just when I was about to go back inside the girl who'd picked me up earlier came out and put her hand on my back in way that was supposed to seem like she hadn't even noticed she was doing it—I could feel it's warmth, for a second it made me feel like I wanted to go straight to sleep—and said that she and the three guys were going down to a café in a suburb just outside the city, a place open twenty-four hours that only cooked two or three things and they were all excellent, she asked me if I wanted to come and I said yes.

"I only really warmed up properly when we got to the café. The air inside was literally wet with the flavors of the cooking food, the bits of nutrition or shit lost in the frying moved around us as moisture in the air and clung to you, but it was warm. I ordered what they ordered and while we waited for the food everybody was a bit quiet and I said to myself in my head *Nicola, you have to keep going* as if I had to run through to dawn and onwards without stopping. Then I laughed a bit to myself, thinking it was going to be impossible, that I'd probably start the slow moody walk home straight after this, get in, open my laptop …

"And then one of the guys said to me, *you should come to the bar with us for another drink, a last drink—it's a great bar—dangerous and funny.*

"When we got there it was just like they said, dangerous and funny—it was obvious from outside that it was a kind of gangster bar, on the second floor of an apartment, all blacked out with a small sign with the place's name on it—a bar that was originally intended for the dangerous members of a single ethnic group but—and this is where the funny part comes in— because it was coincidentally near that area where all the hip bars have been opening up it had also started attracting these small pockets of party kids who you could tell probably had one friend amongst them who could actually drink properly, a guy who, because he knew how to drink, had probably ended up in this bar or one like it once, by accident, just looking for somewhere to keep drinking, and in there he had kept it together in a way that tough guys are inclined to not have a problem with—and so this kid, who could at least hold his drink even if he probably looked as stupid as all his friends, went home and told all his friends about the edgy kind of place he'd started going to and bit by bit they also started coming, getting slipped the wrong change and not really minding, sitting in the corner saying amongst themselves *this place is so cool, did you see that guy*, but rarely being stupid enough to try to mix.

"That was the kind of atmosphere there.

"First all five of us had a shot of vodka at the bar and then one of the guys and the girl left. So it was just three of us left, we sat down in a small booth, they looked bored. These guys drink from physical stamina not emotional stamina. I started drinking much more slowly, big gulps occasionally to look like I was keeping up. One of the guys got up and went to the bathroom, the other to buy some more drinks. When they left I realized I was panicking. I felt much older. I also realized I wouldn't have even told my closest friend that I was panicking in that moment.

"Do you know what it feels like to constantly throw yourself brutally into all this shit you see in front of yourself, into all your anxiety, so completely unobserved, over and over again?

"When they came back to the table, I finished the last drink pretty quickly then left. I went outside and there were some noises starting up and the light in the east was more yellow-blue now. It was magical. I went home quickly in a cab because I didn't want to take my time and lose myself in useless thoughts. The driver raced through back streets, taking a convoluted route just for the pleasure of steering the car through it stiffly. The motor sounded like one you get on a rally car, blowing off its high notes as he gunned it. When I got back to the motel I felt calm again, I felt healthy and focused. I didn't need to go to sleep. I sat in my armchair like I was in a detective movie and every noise I could hear outside meant they were all looking for me and didn't know where to find me."

After a while though, several months, maybe even more than half a year, he stopped making the phone calls. He reached an almost imperceptible breaking point with them, he realized that he no longer took any pleasure in the calls—he no longer liked the way he made the person become so taken with him, the way they ended up having to give themselves up to the long lines of emotion running from him.

This didn't stop him from going out, from frequenting the same bars, or the same kinds of bars in different cities—places where he had become no small expert at finding, no matter where he was, by way of a kind of thinking somewhat akin to the telepathic techniques the military experiments with; using some buried logic of his, some insect-like instinct, to flow through architecture, to walk—walk above all, great big walks through the city, well aware that its old geography was that of many villages, islands separated by seas of disease and poverty, not a sprawling city—collecting all the information he passed like a futuristic detective machine, to find these spots of action, these physical locations that synchronized with the way he wanted to think.

There are texts of his from this period, which at the very least claim to be about this period.

They are all the same, there is no evidence of any experimentation, though a close examination would probably reveal a growing confidence with the techniques, although he never, in any way, lost his humility.

They are all pieces of fiction written in a sort of easy punk-gonzo style, obviously antagonistic to the establishment, wherever the author may locate it on each occasion, but at the same time easy to race through, satisfying the reader's desire pornographically, with the kind of lurid details that overstylize the situation, like an art film that apes a genre intelligently, using the iconicity of character and place to its own cunning ends.

The pieces detail a fairly typical, quiet self-demolition, where the character journeys further and further away from his life to the point where he can no longer recognize which life is his to lose.

This leads to quiet deaths at the end of the pieces. The main character/narrator dies in a way that suggests not only did he not realize that he was approaching death (as opposed to the death of a lifestyle, or set of terms, or idea), but also, at the same time, that he has been forgotten by everyone else, so his mistake becomes irrelevant on a broader scale as well, completely undramatic. The death makes barely a ripple. The narrative twist, for the average reader at least, occurs when you realize the man telling the story is recounting it from beyond the veil of death.

The protagonists of Nicola's stories are always obviously based on himself and the quality of observation is similarly obviously a metaphor for the writer nailing his intellect down within himself, obscuring it from the surface.

This is the immediately apparent operation, Nicola's desert job, the assassination of his past. On this level the texts are easy to understand, in themselves they reveal nothing, on the page he has already wiped the slate clean, everything is shiny and anonymous.

Several of these texts pop up on the internet, on sites hosted by different countries, translated badly, or untranslated, or available exclusively in a language Nicola doesn't even speak. It seems like he's deliberately left them there, left them behind, there, talking to the map. But beyond that, nothing.

While the texts are obviously revisionist (regardless of whether they were written there or later), the successful execution of a plan, not the recording of an experience—if they speak of an experience, it is one he has already resolved to use in a certain manner—there is, at the same time, oddly, incongruously almost, a very superficial expression of a pain he is beginning to feel. Is the surface not the best place to hide things?

Maybe there exists a temporal parallel between the first appearance of this death of the narrator and his decision to end his time overseas, the desert job done (or at least he thought it was done then, though soon after he'd find out it wasn't). He would have begun to wonder how he was going to get home. Whether or not this question struck him suddenly or gradually one cannot know, but, like any person who leaves without imagining a future because, like a criminal, he's too euphoric with the sensation of leaving, he would have been struck, at least momentarily, by a fear that is borderless.

For a moment he would have felt that he would never be able to go home. That there was nowhere he could live but exactly where he was then.

In his motel room, continuously going to check the shades as the sun came up after one of those nights that he didn't think ought to end yet, his mind would have started barking at him angrily *what were you thinking coming here?*—his first reaction to this outburst would have been to look around to see if anyone was there who would notice his distress. His first thought was of being caught in that situation of panic.

He would have tried to keep the whole thing as quiet as possible.

Then, assured that this moment was the correct one, he would have turned his eyes slightly inwards, he would have sat down. Then he would have begun to listen.

Outside, at that hour, he would have heard all kinds of different noises, noises that were occurring for all different reasons: people returning home from parties, some waking up and putting their coffee machine on the stove, two motorbikes racing each other up a long straight strip of nearby road, cats breaking open a garbage bag left outside a restaurant, rats waiting behind the corner—there would not yet have existed, amongst all these different elements, a consensus to begin the day.

He would have only said one thing aloud to himself that morning, only made a single noise, after having sat there for a while. He said, with vain pleasure as he instantly saw from what position he was saying it, as the expression jumped out of him and he felt its wonderful potency:

"I need to get the fuck out of here."

He wouldn't have moved a muscle.

The expression would have reverberated in his thoughts, through his motionless body, thrilling him, intoxicating his intellect; when he had said it the expression had contained its full drama, terrifying, real, empowering.

As he lingered in the delicious drama of what he had just said, he would have understood quickly that he didn't really need to leave, that that wasn't the point, what had actually happened was that as he said those words he had come into a new kind of power; he had acquired the ability to use the metaphor of a kind of movement, the metaphors of exile, of escape, return, secrecy, ambush, etc.

He could take all the time in the world, he now saw, to understand what leaving might mean, how to make it work best, how to model and refine the gesture, how to perfect its form. Only then would he depart.

Realizing this, he would have slouched in his chair a little more comfortably, feeling like he suddenly had a set of extremely valuable objects with him in the room: a small elegant black box full of knives made from the finest steel or luxurious Swiss-made watches, so valuable they could be considered heirloom pieces in even the richest families: the greedy excitement, basically, that one feels immediately after acquiring, through what one likes to call good fortune, enormous wealth.

While the criminal's most common fantasy is of leaving the city, he rarely thinks about returning—except for the bloody vengeful return, which is irrelevant and unrealistic, an aberration of the pure criminal's manner: the pure criminal is concerned that the appearance of things never changes and for that reason has exited the surface of life (a surface on which he may be recognized as a criminal, his activity as illegal). There are few examples of the criminal's quiet return, a few films in which the criminal comes home, out of hiding, quietly slipping back into the boroughs of his past, visiting not the big timers he used to do business with but more modest personalities, a neighbor, a child he used to speak to, now grown up. Then walking the streets in the shadows, in some kind of disguise, returning to pure observation, watching the mechanism operate, reacquainting himself with the routines of the place, noting how they've changed, what to be careful of now. Nothing glamorous enough for Nicola, basically.

6

What becomes clear the more one looks, is that at some point he decided to go home but, subsequent to this realization, this acquired metaphor as he saw it, he made the further decision to delay coming home, more precisely he planned (carefully, or in a last ditch effort, it's impossible to say) a detour.

A detour, an extra splash of alienation or whatever it was he was doing at that point. He gave himself enough time to make it really stink—his decision to come back, to sniff at it and see what it was about it that stank so much—about four months or so, it seems. Four months of conscious detour, almost certainly all spent in China.

Four months or so in another foreign hovel ("a crack house without crack," he wrote to somebody describing his accommodation) counting down the time to his return with a strange aching in his body, a desire, that he left untouched, to cry about himself, intoxicated by what it felt like to be about to leave this—this—whatever he saw all around that so animated him, the sudden blankness of both his past and future probably.

He took the time to visualize his return leading up to it. He sat around in bars, cafes, airports and fantasized about all the ways one could do it.

In the airport before his flight to China, euphoric because of this strange delay he'd offered himself, he felt like he could walk through walls, that's how smooth he thought the way he was walking was, and the silence with which he was doing it (he recollected a French war film where the Resistance members could only parachute back, or take a submarine in and out of their base, as if the world was divided up by enormous unscaleable walls: the potent geographical metaphors of war), and the absolute minimum of luggage he was carrying, and the way he carried it, on his back, making it invisible from certain angles. He was wearing baggy drawstring-waist trousers made from loose linens for travelling comfortably, underneath, though, he felt greasy and dirty, as if he hadn't cleaned behind his scrotum in more than a week.

He arrived at the airport early and went through customs immediately. He roamed the long hallways looking at the different destinations—Istanbul, Porto, Beirut, New York, Qatar—and then walked to the gate of whichever one took his fancy, making out as though he was about to get on the flight. He even watched to see how one might really do it; security at that point wasn't too tight, the personnel not necessarily attentive, people used to get away with amazing things in airports less than fifteen years ago and perhaps all it took to do it again was some brave fantasy.

Then at the last moment, he turned away and sat in a seat at the next gate and thought about what he'd just tried to do and tried to explain to himself how exhilarating it had felt.

Then he got up and with a gluttonous hunger he walked through the complex, deliberating deliciously slowly over where he was going to get a meal that could be as expensive as he liked; he'd order all the sides and trimmings he didn't permit himself in the outside world.

He saw an extremely long queue at the line for transit flights and wondered what it would be like to go to the airport with a partner, somebody with whom he could take turns standing in the slow boring line while the other sat down and read or went to look at the prices of whiskey.

In the end he eventually arrived at his own gate, only ten minutes or so before boarding, and obviously there wasn't a single seat left in the waiting area, so he sat on the floor in a corner, and again started to think about how he was going to go back.

As he sat, trying to keep his back straight, eating the plain sandwich he'd decided on eventually, exhausted by imagining his perfect meal, he stewed on his own cowardice at going back. "I've got the eyes of a coward," he thought, "they always look like they're fucking concentrating." Then he closed these eyes and imagined an artist he had admired, studied hard, tried to emulate on appropriate occasions, feeling the contours of his decision-making process; he imagined the great ongoing process of decisiveness this person lived in, he imagined this decisiveness and he saw himself no longer going in its direction.

He took his suitcase with him to China, the same soft-bodied chic black piece he'd been hauling around since he left Milan, along with a small black backpack made from the finest goat's leather which a friend had sent to him in LA from Japan (LA had been the first time in his life he'd faced the Pacific and the bag had become a personal reminder of this, shot over that body of water to him). In it, along with his best designer clothes, which looked better and better the more clothing he discarded around them as he continued on the trip—on his bed in the hotel he pulled them out a bit and touched the various different pieces, the crisp Japanese rayon of baggy black overcoat, a rubberized wool, heavy but soft nylon, ten-year-old dense polyamide that was bleeding color; they seemed like the work of geniuses who, terrifyingly, hadn't set a limit to their technical evolution, their designs ever more needlessly complex to the point that they now seemed to teeter in front a mirror of creativity's pointlessness; these were objects, he thought, which had been amongst the very first to suffer the burden of an extreme competitiveness—in it, along with the clothes were his books, the small portable library he'd accumulated since leaving home (he'd left Milan with just a few magazines, in a plastic bag, which he used as a carry-on on the first flight). They fell attractively out of the soft suitcase that lay on the hotel bed unzipped like an animal whose delicate underbelly had been slit, spilling a rich and luxurious blood. All these books were annotated and underlined—something he hadn't used to do. He hadn't used to do it because he'd taken too much pleasure in the immaculate consumption of one book after the other, the vain and efficient accumulation of his personal bibliography, as if they were a list of personal victories.

In Mexico City and Los Angeles, though, he'd trashed his books, or he'd tried to improve them, make them more useful to himself, he'd treated them like travelers or ideas incarnated.

In the back of a book of light Italian philosophy there was a jealous love letter he'd written to/about somebody he'd met who'd liked him for reasons he could in no way understand—infuriating him, prompting him, head full of explanations from the book, to write the letter on the back page—though he'd never reread it.

There was an enormous bloody pseudo-detective novel he had reread two and a half times, each time only very vaguely able to remember having read it before, in fact huge sections had been a complete blank to him, so he'd started underlining the sentences which described moments that could have been mistaken, quite literally, for thoughts from his own head. Often these were very banal, like sitting in a hotel room chair wondering where the other people you worked with were staying while on this job if not here in the same place as you. Other times they were more emotional. Sometimes they were physical events he thought might have actually also happened to him, like eating dinner over the kitchen sink so as to not disturb all the carefully arranged reading material you have open on your dining table to different but connected (like you're trying to solve a puzzle) pages.

There were also two books he'd read at the same time, trying to criss-cross chronologies between them with arrows, colored tabs of paper and notes only relevant to specific page numbers in the other book, as if they had been two correspondents—one who never responded to any questions of the other but to whom the other nevertheless continued to write, in fact wrote longer and longer letters, more pathetic and more irrelevant each time, sometimes bitter and angry about the nonresponses like a spurned macho teenage lover with a sensitive streak (a sensitive streak which belongs exclusively to their youth), other times full of mature understanding of all the impossibilities tied up in this kind of articulation. The books, spread out on his bed like loot, had these messy kinds of memories and, more visibly, extruding notes and attempted physical modifications of other kinds.

But he decided to put the books away almost immediately, zipping up the suitcase and throwing it into the closet because there was nothing worse, he reasoned, than being surrounded by his achievements in any form whatsoever. Even though he did this, he found that, with that particular kind of time on his hands, he started making mental lists of all the fiction he'd read while he was overseas, trying to remember other books he hadn't been able to bring with him, that he'd been lent and given back or lent to people in those rare cases in which his enthusiasm for his own private pleasure had spilled out into a conversation that in some way resembled sincerity (he remembered the words literally tumbling out of him one night to an older couple with nuanced sexual attractiveness, tumbling out much the same way those books had tumbled out of his bag, a veritable mess of emotions).

He looked, without realizing it, for patterns in this list, though the only one he became consciously aware of was that none of the writers wrote from cultural capitals of their times. They lived in them for a time, then moved out and began writing seriously, one wrote from a peripheral town, near a capital, within a train ride's distance; another wrote in the middle of nowhere, from various obscure African outposts; another wrote in brief sporadic bursts on rare successful trips just south of the border.

After he got off from work—which more or less consisted of privileged intelligent white people speaking with intelligent Asian people about what was theoretically happening to the city and what theoretically would be done to it in an ideal world—he would let himself go, finding the places that were easiest to find, the bars he was expected to enter, the bars that had the feeling, sickeningly, of having been "discovered" by almost every person with the same background as he who had ever visited the city. At first this meant just one or two bars, then in time three of four, then five, before he hit a limit beyond which he could not easily explore. So he alternated between the five bars, not surprised to see how easily the people like him found other people like themselves to speak to each night, people they vaguely knew, friends of friends.

Here, one night at one of these bars—the one closest to the port area—he overheard an Asian Australian man around his age talking somewhat exasperatedly to a good-looking young white couple, also roughly the same age.

Initially the conversation sounded like the gossipy scandalized pseudo-philosophy that inevitably came out when creative people read things like the *Financial Times* or the *Economist*; the flagrant pragmatism of the articles inspiring in them a series sophisticated psychological insights regarding the dominant consciousness of the times—listening to them, capitalism sounded like a mental disease. The couple continued trying to ask the young Asian man what he thought people there felt about "what's happening."

Nicola listened, his back to their booth, staring at the plants illuminated by green and purple lights in each of the bar's corners.

Their conversation, particularly the couple's insistent questioning, made him remember why everyone loved coming to this city so much; that mental rush of thinking they were somewhere that was both overly speculated on and at the same time unseen, without an image. A pleasurable equation, he thought with distaste.

At some point, the Asian Australian, who, from what Nicola could hear, was drinking far less than the others despite their light mocking, said to them:

"You know I'm stuck here, don't you?"

They laughed: "No." "What!?," more laughter.

"When I first came here, from Australia, it wasn't like I was coming home. I'd never been here before, or only briefly, for family holidays, the usual, you know. So when I came here it was like a foreign land to me, or like I was embarking on an adventure, a new adventure, but obviously I was better equipped than other foreigners who came here, I spoke the language, I looked Asian and so on."

"So anyway," he continued, "when I came here I thought, because of these advantages, I thought it was a once in a lifetime opportunity, you know, to grapple with foreignness with these tools, with these advantages, ready to immediately note the difference in the smell of the air—if I'm going be poetic about it.

"I thought this was the one and only time I'd be so well-equipped, and basically that I had to make the most of it. I felt under pressure, I kept saying to myself *this is your only shot,* though at what I can't remember, or I should say I've never really tried remembering, too busy with other things."

"And what happened? Have you made it? Did you make it? Where are you now?" the girl asked.

The Asian Australian laughed. Then he said: "I've realized now that it's actually not something I have a single shot at, or that the single shot needn't be rushed, that it won't get away from me, that I have no other ambitions than this one, that it's probably going to be the ongoing search of my life—that feeling I had when I first got here—that it wasn't just some hysteria of my early twenties. I think I'm going to be here forever, with the same feeling I had when I got here, more or less, always dealing with the same problem."

Again the girl, eager, jumping at his pause for breath or a sip of his drink, asked him another question, almost whining in her insistence on desiring the right answer: "But what ambition? What do you mean this one ambition? The same feeling?"

He smiled again.

First he said: "I don't know."

Then he said, "To drift. The feeling of drifting."

Nicola, when he heard the word, felt a stab of panic; he wasn't going to move but he felt cold all over. He was sweating and it smelt particularly strong, of all the toxins that hadn't been secreted since he last did any sport, months ago.

When he heard the word he remembered himself cut off from his own future.

He wanted to turn around and see this man's face.

To drift is to realize that you could stay on, he knew, residually, after something ends—maybe not even as a residue of something of your own, but as a trace of anything you can find that has the potential for a residue—maybe take on another job, remain unknown, maybe never wake up again from this disturbed dream that began to take you over as you forgot or neglected your motives, maybe slowly crumble and not mind—ambition dissipating into the landscape—to not be humiliated by this failure, but instead be overjoyed that you've found a way to do it so numbly and at the same time so poetically—drifting is basically, he thought, to disappear from a certain surface of life: the art of losing purpose.

How it all ended after this is unclear, the plane he caught, where he re-entered, who was there to greet him, in what state of mind he was, what he was wearing, what he'd eaten (if anything), if he'd tried to grow his hair a little again, if he had been doing physical activity or if his body was soft, if there were dimples in the flesh underneath his biceps from lack of exercise, or if they were toned and articulate.

All that is known, though, is that at a certain point he is no longer in China and he is no longer considered to be "living abroad." The dates for this vanishing correlate with the dates of the last texts written with the dead narrator. Successive to this, the online trace of him becomes chronologically scattered and unclear. At some point, later enough to make one a little uneasy, he pops up again, as if he'd always been there but nobody had noticed, as an established member of Milan's most successful young movers and shakers, lecturing on how Italians ought to do business, holding an important position in a multinational company, admired by a younger generation who, painfully confused, can't understand the black sea between him and them, how to become him. There is no story of the rise to power, no reasons given for the sudden high esteem in which he is held by almost everyone. The stories that one can find are mockingly formulated myths of some kind of superhuman able to do everything—from professional hip-hop dancing to high-level art collecting to government budgeting—all within a questionably short time period. In fact it is with regard to time above all that his past seems murky in the official stories that appear. It seems as though he hasn't progressed through it so much as used dates as signposts, when it pleased him, as if he had been living forever.

7

At some point meeting in the city becomes too tense, unbearably tense; the idea of trying to see him in Milan seems absurd. I leave my phone untouched. I want to see him but at this point I can't think of any excuse significant enough to convince him. A sense of desperation advances in my thoughts, hiding it seems impossible.

I can't compete with his Milanese priorities, I want to impinge upon him as little as possible. I feel ridiculous, any gesture towards him feels too stark.

If we're going to speak we have to speak unobserved, I decide. I need to speak to him in the place where he thinks, not where he enacts his decisiveness, a place where the city is invisible other than how it appears to us in our imaginations.

From one piece or another of stolen or mistakenly handed down information (nobody thinks I know anything here, their circles of friendship never overlapping, they confide in vagaries to me, not realizing I know exactly what they refer to) I find out when he's going to be away and I make my plans to be there at the same time, always, seemingly, gently encouraged by him.

Sometimes, on my way to see him, logic cedes to something less precise, perhaps more useful, I see him and I in some kind of abstract formation: we are an accumulation of geographies, sometimes lapping over each other like waves as they hit the shore and get sucked back out again, sometimes connecting, sometimes antagonizing each other. And in this gradual accumulation that we form, I see my only chance for moving forward, moving forward in a city where I've suddenly been caught without a purpose.

And so I meet him elsewhere—we stay away from each other in Milan—I meet him in London once on a Sunday or Saturday morning—I'm at the bar I arranged to meet him in, drinking a disgusting Bloody Mary (I'd somehow remembered, wrongly obviously, that it was a cult drink in this place). He arrives as if he's come on foot, he says something to me about the night before, something about being in a basement, only coming up every now and then to get phone signal (I'd tried to call him). He mentions a residential area on the perimeter of the latest best area for going out at night, a zone just beyond all the lights and noise and clumps of sudden density of those nightclubs, an area where the sound from the nearby nightspots seems to fall, literally, on deaf ears.

I look at him. The stubble on his head seems particularly soft, almost like tufts of cashmere. He tells me he likes my "little jacket" ("*bella tua giachetta*"). When he speaks to me it sounds as though he has two precious black marbles behind his molars that slur his words ever so casually (almost imperceptibly) as they come out giving them a strange smooth richness.

He accepts my suggestion to eat at a nearby restaurant, a place with exceptional light. Inside, very few of its furnishings—the tables, the chairs, the stacks of glasses, the salt and pepper shakers—seem to rise above waist level, leaving an uninterrupted horizontal plane of sleekness, giving the impression of constant silent bustle just slightly below the level of one's vision.

The light pours in from the long horizontally rectangular windows in a way that's only possible in England, full of melancholy arousal, a light that seems to have an opaque consistency, initially, breaking down into many smaller parts as the day progresses (a slow breaking of the spirit seemingly, an Englishman waking up with a hangover next to a full white naked body in stuporous awe, walking to the bathroom to pop a pimple and piss, tight calf muscles, bare feet slapping the cold concrete).

He orders as though he were hung over himself: bacon and beans and lamb's tongue, but acts the same as he always does. We have beers instead of wine (we always prefer beers to wine, as though the color suits us better, that uncertain brown).

We begin speaking intimately, we exchange ideas, the conversation has a subtly strategic air, as though we are planning something here, looking back to Milan, as though we are arranging elements for a more efficient approach once we get back to the city. I look at him in that clean light, I feel my knuckles and fingers, which had been cold outside, burning a little on the surface as their circulation starts improving.

At some point two of his companions from the previous night, an older man and young woman, arrive at the restaurant. They hand off their enormous, expensive but shabby coats to the waitress in a manner that suggests she needn't bother asking them where they're going to sit or what they'll be ordering.

They bring an air, again gently, of thuggishness to the restaurant as they sit a little more sprawled than the other guests, their legs a little more in the way of the waitresses, a little more of a risk to them should they move too briskly between tables. They eat what is left of what Nicola and I ordered, taking the plates across to their side as if it were an automatic procedure.

Nicola and my conversation continues through them, actually it takes a heightened turn. He uses the girl's questions to reveal himself to me. I don't say anything, placidly removed in glacial observation. For the first time since I've known him he speaks of himself precisely and honestly.

She makes general conversation: "Why are you here, exactly, Nicola?" "What kinds of things do you get up to in Milan?" "What are you boys all about?" He replies from a strange stillness (somehow making very normal questions seem monumental): "Hustling, hustling," he chuckles, "Dangerous stuff," "Power," "Do you think we do those things for any reason other than the fact that it's what we really like doing? People, they would realize it in a second if we didn't," in that soft English of his, his eyes glistening in my direction.

It all seems so starkly obvious when he says it; it's everything I'd imagined was in his head.

When the check arrives he reaches for it immediately without rushing, with only his hand moving. The rest of his body, even his eyes, remain still.

He pays and I look at him and say: "Nicola, thank you." He looks at me gently and says: "No, thank you."

There are a few more of these meetings: brief, profound only for what they are, rather than what happens during them which is, essentially, nothing; an exchange of expressions, a fragmentary flickering of the eyes and shifting of a gaze away from its initial target.

They all come to a head, a finale, during one such meeting near Bologna.

"The difference between me and you," I tell him, in this, perhaps the last (or was it the only?) long conversation we ever have, in a small restaurant in the backroom of a grocery store just outside Bologna, "the difference between me and you is that I don't go back. I won't allow myself the option." For the first time in the conversation he doesn't seem to object to what I've said and this makes me glow a little inwardly, still believing even then that maybe we could be partners in dreams one day.

In that conversation the world seems to have finally peeled off its turgid layer. I couldn't imagine what was going to happen next, now that we were together.

He tells me about his lies. "I kept my intellect separate," he says. "I always felt uneasy going out, though I kept doing it." To hear these things spoken was magical.

He gives no reasons for telling me what he tells me. I wonder if he was trying to help me in some strange way. I want to tell him I've known everything he is saying almost from the beginning, but as he speaks, he refuses to acknowledge my complicity in what he is saying.

Instead he gives me advice assuming I am desperately asking for it. He makes no allowance for the personal nuances of my situation, he makes no effort to find alternatives or shades of his decisive opinions that might coexist with my circumstances, that might cooperate. He seems to accuse me unreservedly of everything he feels he has overcome, indiscriminately placing moments of his life on top of what he imagines mine to be.

He says to me, absurdly, at some point, as I check the clock on the wall behind his head—almost three thirty—hardly believing he has agreed to suspend his life for so long in this little backroom, just to speak to me, asking myself "are we entering that zone where things don't stop?" and "is this love?"—he says to me:

"You: you are just frustrated because you want people, here, when you enter the room, to already know who you are, you want them to say *ah he is the guy who did that, who did this*—that's your problem."

A cosmic joke.

I want to tell him everything has changed and nobody has noticed. I want to say "when I'm with you I realize I want to be nothing, I want to give and receive the same things, even in their extremes, passive or dominant, I slide easily between the roles, my satisfaction doesn't lie in the action, I just want to feel—feel the map, feel what you feel when you act or when, silently, you can't, when you are unable to feel anything. I realize I can like anything, I'm loose, I don't need to define myself anymore, actually it's become impossible, the path I make through life, hardly believing it, always quietly surprised, has lost all consistency."

But instead I just look at him—genuinely bewildered, I think—wondering what slip of the tongue, what trick, what idiocy this is. What vengeful retribution for what had come before? What fear? What plan?

8

One day we meet in one of the offices he uses in Milan. We meet under the pretext of work. The office is at the back of a large conceptual retail store. This rear section, not open to the public, is done in a similar style to the store itself; Brutalist concrete, polished to a deadened gloss with aluminium bolts, probably of no actual functional use, occasionally visible in corners of the concrete rectangles. But the space he's using at the back is empty of merchandise or decorations except for a couple of old promotional posters for events that have been held there, though they are in the corner and barely catch my eye. In this emptiness there are two cheap thin-legged bar tables and stools. He is alone, on his computer, working at one of the two tables. He looks like he's dressed for the beach. He greets me as though I'm just another blot in the landscape sliding past him. "Eyy ciao," he says quietly, quietly but clearly, as if at exactly the same volume and consistency with which he was articulating his own private thoughts to himself before I arrived—so that there might be no change whatsoever in his manner, literally no emotional acknowledgement. It would probably be impossible for anyone to look less surprised.

I say "ciao" to him as well and it feels as if the situation could drift right back into silence after I say it. He makes no effort to move towards a normal conversation. I can't think of anything normal to say myself, not to him. With almost immediate desperation I try to think of something we have in common I might never have mentioned before, some new common ground we could open up. Nothing much comes to mind so I draw at my surroundings, I mention a jacket I saw in the store on my way through to see him, a sort of hip varsity jacket in the colors of the Brazilian football team rather than the usual blacks, greys, and burgundies.

I tell him I like it, trying to provide, through my reasons, an insight that could be representative of the culture around that type of clothing in general.

"*Volgare, forte, heh-heh, un tipo di fuck-you divertente … quante ne avete fatte? … Mi posso immaginare i tipi qui che la vorebbero comprare.*"

He responds as if I've said I think the jacket is some kind of stain on my imagination.

He says, contrarily, "I was thinking of doing one for myself."

"Yeah yeah, I mean I think it's wild in a good way, I mean somebody like you could really make it work," I say, trying to take the momentum of conversation, as contrary and awkward as it is, trying to open it up.

After this, he warms up slightly and starts telling me about a new jacket, a work in progress that he's now having embroidered for himself.

At first I misunderstand and think that it's a piece he's designed, a limited edition, a punk emblem of the city that he wants to sell to a few powerful men and a few gullible kids. I ask him how many he's having made.

"You crazy? Just one. It cost me €500, fuck."

"Just one, why just one?"

"It's for me, it's my personal jacket. It's got all my references, the things people know me by, my hotel room number I always take, my old nickname, the logo of my most famous blog from when I was in LA …"

We talk about the colors in which to do it, he's undecided whether to do black on black or not.

I tell him that black on black, or any tone-on-tone branding detail has *rotto il cazzo*, that there is nothing more mundane than this timid expression of discretion and good taste, pink on black, I tell him, pink and green on black and a dash of orange under the ribcage, imagining it as a whole story, getting excited for a moment …

"No no, but you know, because of the subject matter," he says, referring to some obscene language included in the embroidered words.

Then we talk about the inside of the jacket, I ask him if he could put some wild lining in there, thinking of something special I could recommend to him, he tells me it doesn't have a lining, that style of jacket, but now that I mention it he might embroider some other things on the inside.

We continue to talk a little more and I offer a few further suggestions. Then at some point, discussing some jackets with similar style, old pieces to be found occasionally on Ebay, the issue of size comes up.

"What do you take?" he asks me.

"Well it depends, you know, buying vintage from different countries they take different measurements."

"And what do you need to know from me to get me one?"

"Well there in the UK they use pit-to-pit."

"Pit-to-pit?"

"From one armpit of the closed jacket to the other. And they want it in inches. I'm a 21", sometimes 22" depending on the lining, 23" if it's something very special, a must have."

He looks at me.

"Well I'm bigger than you," and it's true, I'd never realised. I look at him more closely, perhaps I even squint my eyes. From the way he held himself I'd never realized. His shoulders are almost broad. I'd more or less taken it for granted that we were the same size.

After leaving I cross the road and walk towards my place. I have a good twenty-minute walk ahead of me. I keep thinking about his new jacket, even though I haven't seen it, I think I know what he's talking about, I think I know why he wants one, what he's doing with it—I want one for myself. As I walk I imagine myself wearing it, with all Nicola's layered symbols, I imagine myself wearing it overseas, in some other city, slipping into his history, not being bothered to be myself, sitting in, getting by just by doing what he did, just doing a Nicola, let everything else go.

I imagine traveling around as some version of him, occasionally falling into imitations of him at bars, unnoticed, other times putting on jokey performances for people who vaguely remember him.

I imagine myself in LA in a bar, at the back where the ceiling becomes lower, somebody saying to me "Is that Nicola's jacket you're wearing?"—and me doing that silent laugh of his while at the same time leaning forward a little and sliding my arm away from my body to reveal a bit of the jacket's lining.

Maybe signing some articles in his name somewhere, using his old blogging handle, using stories (true or imagined) from his past as flat lies to amuse myself when meeting new people, whatever slides off the tongue easiest. Knowing that in the face of fear I only have to remember to mimic him. "What did you do in Milan?" "I ran a *porno* magazine." A light laugh, my eyes holding the same gaze.

"Anything he can do I can do," I tell myself, believing it sincerely, somewhat moved by the truth of the statement I've made to myself … It is true, a profound realization, another shifting of the ground underneath my feet.

And it's with these thoughts in mind when I get home that I begin tracking a few of his recent online movements which I'd bookmarked the night before, a few blogs he's linked posts from, some songs he's recommended. Still excited, as I check the traces, about my thoughts taking over some part of him overseas with the jacket, I come across what I think is another writer who is writing about him in the city. A delicious fear immediately overtakes me. It's a blog written by a girl of a geographically inconsistent background; American, Eastern European, big city, small city, hipster, spy ... it's very hard to discern. It's a blog where she writes about her notable sexual encounters, all sorts of different encounters in different cities, but mostly in Milan. One piece in particular, about a sado-masochistic relationship with an Italian man, catches my eye; some details seem vaguely familiar. The piece itself is anony-mously written. Because of the delicate nature of the subject matter the writer never gives her name, so we don't who the author is exactly. The names of all the characters are avoided, but, and my suspicions begin in earnest here, I recognize the internal structure of the apartment in which she conducts the relationship—I run through the text a second time, more meticulously, noting only the movements of the characters through the flat, between dining room, bathroom, bedroom, making a mental map, and yes the apartment could be his, Nicola's. And other things I noticed subconsciously on the first reading start making sense too. I study the piece several more times extremely closely, I rack my memory for things he's said and done. Yes yes, there is no doubt her lover is Nicola.

"The good thing about her is you can't tell where she's from." I remember him telling me at a bar about someone I didn't think I knew.

This girl writes about things that, as far as Nicola's image is concerned, never happened—and this makes me nervous as I sit in front of the computer, reading material freely available to the public, with nothing but a genuine curiosity; they are the zones one never sees in him. It dawns on me that these things she described actually happened with him, in Milan. And later, as I begin to attach his face to the action, I grow perturbed.

"It's there!" I shout at myself in front of the glowing computer screen. "The dark underbelly of the city, the nightlife, the low lifes, the action, the moment when the city becomes something you can gorge on, a place you walk through and make shit happen, for god's sake!!!"

It's the first hard evidence I've found of thousands of things I've believed since I met him, the most extraordinary things, the purest things. Impossible to describe beyond this.

That night I sleep badly, I have dark vague visions of scenarios in which I'm supposed to engage with him but can't, where he gives me the opportunity to do something with him (I can only vaguely remember what) and I find that I'm incapable. In these visions, a mix between sleep and what does not allow you to sleep, what torments you in half-sleep, I see myself with him, with this new knowledge of his intimate encounters, and I'm trying to convey that I understand something, something about our friendship, about what I know we have in common, but I can't speak it, I keep rubbing up against it, this thing I want to say, growing so increasingly agitated I can't communicate, and at the same time can't fall into peaceful sleep. I wake up fully at some point and tell myself that now it's time to sleep, time to calm down and go to sleep (because I'm too emotionally exhausted to get up and reflect further on the situation), and, having convinced myself, eventually I do.

Whatever she writes seems to completely outstrip, in terms of realism, any of the experiences I've ever shared with him. In the moments when I think about what she's written, a certain kind of life seems definitively out of reach for me:

He buys me a cheap nylon dog collar with a metal chain, which means I'm "his" when I wear it. And I promise to have it with me every time we meet. It works, for the most part.

"Hey baby. You got your collar?"

I'm on my way to my birthday party but stop by his place first. He doesn't want to come because my friends are "junkie club kids." As I stand at the entrance and he checks out my outfit I realize I've forgotten to bring something vital with me.

"Shit."

Shit! Why didn't he ask for it yesterday, when I took a fucking €50 taxi ride to get it? Or when I drag it around in my bag for days to work and school and parties? Now he probably thinks I don't care and now he definitely won't fuck me.

"You're such a bad slave."

Oh, goddamnit.

"I'm sorry."

I remember the last time I forgot my collar—he refused to talk to me all night. Suddenly hot, fat tears start slowly rolling down my face.

"Don't cry baby, come here."

He sits me in his lap.

"You know, sometimes I think this is a game for you."

"It's not," I sob, "I'm just not used to this!"

"Then you have to try harder."

He rips a hole in the crotch of my stockings.

"Now you'll think of me all night."

"Like I wouldn't have already."

He slaps me in the face and sends me on my way—with vodka, for my shitty party.

"Ciao, Bella."

We first met at a classy Milanese porn gig. He was the director that night, and I was the model—only by the end of the shoot he joined me in the spotlight, shoving his fingers in my "Figa D'oro." I fell for him instantly and stalked/pursued him until he finally took me out.

On our first date he takes me to a nasty strip club just outside the city. We go downstairs. He knows all the dancers in the bar and calls them by their names.
　He buys me drinks and pays for a private room at the back, where I decide to hit on him properly.

"I've been masturbating to you for weeks," I slur, already a bit drunk. I wait and wonder if he's heard me because his facial expression hasn't changed. I'm just about to start laughing when he says something.

"I wanna make you my slave."

He says it completely seriously. But I'm too wasted to really get what he means anyway and he's too grossed out by my period to fuck me.

The next morning when I'm sober I want to see him again and can't remember how we left things the night before. So I call him up.
　"So when am I going to come over and be a slave for you?"
　At first he doesn't say anything.

Then he laughs kind of quietly, then he says "Okay Bella, you can be my slave."

We have sex for the first time on a fuzzy red bed in a Swingers' Club outside Milan. I have a good time despite all the voyeurs, but he tells me that he was too nice.

"I fucked you like I would fuck my mother," he says into my ear after I come.

He has me pinned down with his elbow digging into my neck. I feel part of his hairy soft stomach pressed against my ass.

I can only see out to the guys who have been watching us from the side of the bed. Three bored older guys in expensive suits, then a couple of guys I think I've seen at parties before, one really short one with a beard and a baseball cap, another with a curly goatee and crumpled summer suit.

He loosens the pressure a bit. I turn my head as far back towards him as I can and reach his ear, I reply.

"No," I tell him. "It was great!" Then, "I think I'm gonna black out."

I don't remember how or when he leaves. But after that we start seeing each other all the time.

He starts taking me to trendy parties and his favorite bars. We share tons of taxis. He begs me to start eating more so we can go out to dinner. I meet all of the people he says are his friends. They all seem older but still they always call him "capo" or "boss."

He tells me they are "the best men I'll ever find in Milan," whatever that means.

They all try to act like they've seen it all before a million times.

At a bar one night one of them, F., stands at the bar while two people fight next to him. One of the guys throws a bunch and half hits F. accidentally but still he doesn't move. Instead he changes his drink into the hand furthest from the action and just keeps watching without saying anything.

One time, at the end of the night, he takes me up with his friends to a room in the city's most expensive hotel.

"I thought only tourists came here."

He laughs.

"No, Bella, that's just what stupid people think. These rooms are rented out by rich Milanese perverts every night."

He doesn't fuck me in front of his friends, though. He just sits at the table near the window with them and orders drinks. I order a cocktail and pass out after a few sips, bored.

When I wake up he's awake and has ordered a massive breakfast, for at least five people, even though there's only three of us there now and I never eat, as well as a bottle of whiskey and packs of cigarettes.

It's already on the table near the window. He's sitting there with F. who's smoking silently, with his head down, listening to him. He's having some of the whiskey and I can't tell if he's slept.

He's talking to F. about some trip they took to Mexcio City a few months ago, and, for once, he sounds sad.

I feel like shit so I don't say anything. I lie back down and try to go back to sleep.

He calls me from a car in front of my house one day while I'm out with some hot boys. I imagine him in the back of the taxi waiting, dressed in a new baggy suit and big chunky black leather shoes.

I ditch the boys for him. I start feeling attached. The sex gets harder.

"You know, we're just playing like kids now."

"What?"

My face is covered in spit, my ass is red from spanking and my neck is starting to bruise.

"If you're my slave, there's no going back. It's psychological. I'll be your Master even when you're married."

I hate when he talks about me ending up with somebody else.

"I know."

"So you're my slave?"

"Yes."

"For how long?"

"Forever."

Somewhere within these months I find myself in love with this [unavailable] man. He's married and I know eventually he'll just be my friend—and "Master"—if I'm lucky.

I imagine a botoxed, old me meeting him in the expensive hotel rooms dressed in a pink suit and matching pink heels. Though the hotel is amazing I feel as though I am all dried up, like I've gone over some unwritten limit for the number of fucks I can have and that it's his fault. Then he arrives and he looks identical to how he looks now.

Depressing to imagine.

I choose not to think about it. Instead I focus on making him hug me till I fall asleep.

A couple of time he lets me sleep until the morning at his place. Not much light comes into his bedroom. When I wake up he's already up, sitting in the bed, just staring at me. I move close to his arm and smell it. He hasn't had a shower. He doesn't say anything. I reach for the cigarettes, take one, put it in my mouth and light it.

"You don't need a cigarette at eight in the fucking morning."

Yes, I fucking do.

I put it out.

"And please eat something."

He buys me a brioche and we kiss goodbye for work. We're happy. "We'll find a way to make this work," I think. I'm an idiot.

"I wish you were under this desk during my boring meeting." He writes to me.

I get desperate for his texts and we call each other ten times a day. I can't live without knowing where he is every minute. "If you died, I would get arrested," he once remarks on how often we talk. "They'd think I killed you."

I send him thousands of naked pictures of myself ...

"Can I come over later?"

I sit across from him at his table after we finish dinner. I worry that I drank too much—he won't let me pee.

"Get on the floor."

I look up at him as he slaps me, pulls my hair and grabs my face. I wonder what he's thinking. Does he only do this for me? How many "slaves" has he had? I wonder what I look like in that moment.

I look up at him again as he hits me.

After he hits me again I wonder if anybody knows that I come to his flat. It's completely quiet up here, he even has the balcony doors open.

He ties me to a wooden column in his living room, and lets me curl up in the corner. I feel myself relax under his watch and fall asleep to the sound of his breathing as he reads a magazine. Moments (hours?) later, his harsh touch wakes me. He's slapping me again, and now spits in my mouth. He takes off my stockings.

"You are looser," he points out, shoving a beer bottle neck inside me.

"No!"

"Shut up babe."

I realize I'm "looser" because I fucked two other guys that week— a feeble attempt to be less obsessed with him. Predictably I couldn't help but compare them to him the whole time, their tongues felt like sandpaper in comparison when they licked me …

They were put off when I insisted they call me a "slut" and thought it was "sad" how I would flinch whenever they raised their arms—as if it weren't normal for me to expect them to hit me.

"Go to the bathroom and wait."

I go to the other bathroom downstairs past his bedroom.

I lay down naked on the freezing tiles. It feels like hours.

"What the hell is he doing?" "How long will this take?" "I could easily go back up." "No, don't be pathetic." "Do I honestly like this?" "I could cover myself with a towel." "But no, that wouldn't count."

When he finally comes down he's proud to see me waiting. He lifts me up, holds me tightly and gives me a forehead-kiss. He sits me down in his shower.

"Open your mouth."

His piss is warm and I can feel it everywhere. I don't want it to stop.

I wish he'd let me touch myself.

"Look at me."

He watches me shower, dries me off and brings me into his bedroom.

"Sit down."

He ties me up to the arms of his chair and eats my pussy like gelato.

"I wanna be a good slave for you," I tell him.

"Then next time, shave."

I come like a bitch.

"This is the beginning. You need more training. But soon, you will be perfect."

While I lie on the floor and he sits above me we discuss a lot of things. He likes fucking whores—I like being watched—he wants me to suck his dick at a restaurant—I want him to humiliate me in public—he wants to take me to a swinger's club and make me get gang-banged by five other guys.

He unhooks my collar.

"You're free now."

Relieved, tired, and sore, I lie in his bed and think.

I don't know it then, but it's the last time I'll ever sleep with him.

When I wake up the next morning I realize that I'm going to have to meet with him again soon, one way or another. I feel anxious because even then I already feel certain that he knows that I know about this secret relationship of his, that I've discovered what happened, and that he doesn't take kindly to my snooping around, that nobody in Milan dares do that to him. In fact I'm already convinced then that when I do eventually meet him, even though I will reassure myself on some level that there's no way that he can know what I do in the privacy of my own computer, his behavior will confirm my paranoia so absolutely that I will almost even try to mention it to him, try to apologize to him and make light of it, tell him I'm cool with it and that his secret is safe with me, even though, as I keep repeating to myself, there is no way he could possibly know.

I think all this when I wake up, straight away, without a moment of fuzziness or fog. It is all very clear, as I move my legs out of my bed and place them on the cool tiles of the floor and find the underwear I'd slipped out of right there before getting into bed the night before with my toes—it's a completely fateless morning.

Fuck it, I think. Right then, in the face of the situation, I stop caring, I don't give up, I don't decide to make friends with less dangerous people, I don't think I should stop being interested in things that humiliate me—these pathetic thoughts don't even figure with me. I just bluntly erase a kind of caring I used to have.

I start imagining—like some worst-case scenario, some attempt at absolution, at hitting rock bottom without excuses—a future conversation where I describe what happened in Milan to someone, spilling out the pathetic details quickly: "No I had no friends, nothing, in two years. Yes, I failed entirely to create a life for myself there. I never understood anything when I lived there. Zero." Then the other person laughs and I say, "No no no I'm not joking, seriously, it was a complete failure, I achieved nothing." And so on. On my haunches in front of a girl as she sits, trying to lay the whole thing out in the most dynamic way possible, turning it into some kind of routine, making the insights sharper and sharper, searching her face for that openness to absolutes, that flat desperation that allows for a mind to take in the entire vision of someone else, tricks of a drifter … getting myself close to some dangerously sentimental fucks.

It's the kind of morning that one's memory more often than not erases, or judges poorly, as some kind of temporary hysterical necessity, but occasionally, though, things remain as hard and glinty as the moment in which they were first experienced.

That morning, I see I've been painting a paranoid picture in my head of a city you could gorge on, while I lived in the empty one. These are the two strange parallel worlds that the city allows to coexist. This is me and him, side by side, with everything between us.

All of a sudden, in my noncaring, I feel like I don't exist, as if I've been wiped off the map, that when the tension between us was severed I became nothing. I am still there, in the city, but somehow any goals I had have sunken below the ground without a trace or a sound. I'm more than forgotten (because I'd already felt forgotten a long time ago). I'm blissfully without purpose, my interest in being myself has evaporated.

And so, in this state of mind, I write to "Bella"—and I knew who she was, long before the secret came out for everyone else, it didn't take me a moment to fit the racial profile, the scenes described, the kind of English she used—I write to her because more than anything else in those moments, that morning, the night before, I want to know how he felt, I want to know how he felt in as many moments as possible and I think, not entirely lucidly, that I can make her tell me.

"Dear Bella,"—

At first I invent back stories, I distance myself from the city, I try to approach her in another guise, to lose my tail (I'm still paranoid that he may detect me). The stories are wild lies. I tell her I come from Bologna (I'm a professor, a foreigner like her), I'm from Rome (a journalist, a sportswriter, a lonely foreigner trying to navigate the open piazzas of the place with little success), I'm from Taranto (a deviant, an outlaw, a mythological character). Then I begin asking her to tell me something she does not even know yet:

"Dear Bella," I say. "It all sounded like a noir. I imagined detectives in Milan fishing bodies of young women out of canals, trying to pin the murder on Master or his friends."

"Italian men like this … rich, powerful … underground world … did he ever ask you why you were in Milan? Were you ever genuinely afraid?"

"Did he mention fate?"

"Did he keep your relationship a secret?"

"What did you talk about for hours as he stood over you, apart from sex?"

"Did he ever tell you you should leave the city? And go where, in his opinion?"

"He didn't ever mention escape, did he?"

Or in another I try:

"I love the image of you making him hug you as you fell asleep …" I sit in front of this for hours, trying different follow-up questions. How can I ask her how he felt as she made him do this?

I change tack.

I feel exhausted.

In the end I simply write, trying to blandly encompass everything:

"Did he ever show any moments of weakness?"

Writing the messages, the possibility of deception—unfortunately even anonymity still requires deception—contracts to the barest hope.

It was impossible to ask for more. They would have smelled a rat. All the time, no matter what I wrote, I could still feel Nicola watching me, knowing exactly what I was doing in each moment. What I sent in the end was so flat that even he couldn't guessed its long history of motives.

Her answer comes back guarded and aloof, full of lies, basically, even though it's only two lines long, implying things I'm sure never happened.

After this I cease to think about who Nicola really is for a while.

I spend about a month or so in this strange position, in the same city as him, not seeing him, not chancing upon him—our two worlds no longer seem to be running parallel, let alone overlapping. He is doing his thing and I am doing mine. The days no longer seem to glide one into the other, but stop and start in short episodes.

One night I see Gianluca, the actor who doesn't realise he's an actor, again. I'm standing outside a bar and I see him from far away, walking towards the place. He is walking stiffly, as if his chest and shoulders are blocked, he is walking as stiffly as an old person. "He looks like his father," I say to myself aloud with distaste, spitting the phrase out as if it has a bitter taste. But I'm already drunk and I walk towards him. We'd arranged to meet there, though as usual, he's late, and also as usual, won't mention the reasons for this, in the same test he predictably performs with everyone. I greet him enthusiastically, touching his shoulder with my arm and squeezing it more than I ever have before.

He smiles at me, making his eyes shine a little.

We walk in and I get another drink. He just asks for a glass of water, they serve him first, he drinks it quickly in pronounced gulps, he asks for another immediately. The way he asks for it also seems like a test, testing the goodwill of the people who work behind the bar.

I stand close to him, slightly behind, trying to shoulder in to the bar and order my drink. He smells bad. Like a homeless person. The odor seems to be on him the way a fine dirt accumulates on a white station wagon after thousands of fast kilometers on the highway, in irregular patches, as if it's been delicately applied with a fine brush, with a peculiar sheen to it, like a crust.

I think this smell of his is put on, a perfume.

He turns to me and smiles but it's as if I'm oil underneath water, in a world beneath his, sealed from him.

I turn away from his smile, insist with my ribs against the bar and order the drink.

"Where does he want us to think he's been with that fucking smell on?" I think to myself. He wants people to imagine he's kept going, I guess, that he's on and on and on and on. That he's like that white car on the highway, a car that in reality belongs to some vulgar Italian salesman, the classic pony-tailed *commerciale* who listens to techno mix tapes from the moment he starts driving at six a.m. until about five in the afternoon, when he stops at a gas station to hear the commuter traffic … Ignoring the dusk, he drinks a tall Monster energy drink before driving on in a quiet slide to his day's last destination.

Gianluca wants people to think he's been racing through that underworld. But nobody but an idiot has his face and smells like that.

He wants people to think he has a reason for ignoring fatigue.

My drink arrives and maybe I drink it too quickly because he's finished his second glass of water and doesn't look like he's going to ask for a drink that he has to pay for. After a few minutes, he says he's going to another bar for a drink.

"Wait wait," I tell him, "I'll come with you."

I finish up and follow him out.

We walk down one of the canals, across a bridge, then a little further down the next canal, then across another bridge and through some backstreets, and finally out onto a larger road. We follow it down to a small intersection where there's a bar that serves good beer.

We walk in. It's empty, so we can order straight away, I ask what he thinks he's going to have, he looks at me and puts on the same smile he put on in the last bar, and without bothering to note my expression and obviously not remembering my expression last time he smiled at me that way, he says: "Well … since you're offering I'll have a _____," and he names some imported ale they have on tap.

I feel like someone's trying to start a fight with me. I feel a cold rush of adrenaline in my stomach, I feel like I haven't eaten in days, I feel a little shaky.

I smile then laugh with something like a drunken lack of control.

I buy him his drink.

I should have beat the shit out of him, I think, as we stand outside sipping our beers looking around at the few people there that night, or at least tested myself, seen if I'd had the means, in the toilets when he went and took a piss, as he was pissing relaxedly into the urinal, breathing out in satisfaction, lost in his pleasure, with his back to the door as I entered it quickly and quietly, in a flurry of black-clad limbs—that would have been the way to do it.

I'm not saying much and he notices a person nearby looking in our direction so he impatiently starts a conversation, asking them gruffly and quickly, with what is supposed to be a novel and charming frankness, what they do. I'm left standing there, as he turns towards this person. The murmuring life of the people passing by flickers past my eyeballs, I'm still contemplating that feeling of wanting to physically punish Gianluca, I'm turning its satisfactions over in my head, deliberating over them, like the tourist who gets scammed by a nightclub in a foreign city and begins his plane ride home, at the moment he takes his seat, with the thought: "I'm going to go back the next time I have any time off and kill that owner-fucker, end that man's life."

I see Nicola one last time. It's not a particularly special evening. It's at his house, he invites me over through someone else, without even raising a finger probably. When we see each other he makes no mention of everything he must know has come between us. Accordingly, I can't find any reason to behave differently.

He tells me almost immediately that he's about to leave the city, that he's asked for a change in position and he'll be in India or Russia before Christmas. While it's news to me, I also glumly expected it at any moment now. I don't know why he's leaving, I can't imagine what comes next—it will be no help to me anyway.

I don't ask him for the reasons for his decision.

Maybe he's leaving just to see how much it really is his, this empty city, how it's still always within his grasp. He has learned how to enter it, how to leave, and then how to enter it again. He's gotten so used to the motion he's even become attuned to the sound, the "whoosh" the empty city makes when you return. I think all this, not really making any sense, just visualizing his movement, in and out again, in and out of Milan. I can't yet tell what's going to happen that night. Outside on the balcony, the air seems liquid and dense. As usual, there isn't a shred of wind in Milan, and the hot air isn't moving.

The purpose of our meeting is extremely unclear. He'd told somebody he was with to send me a text saying that he, i.e., the other guy, was there, i.e., at Nicola's place, if I wanted to pass by. When I arrived the other guy had left but Nicola let me in anyway, as if he was expecting me. And then he said he'd be gone by Christmas.

I look around the flat and try to deduce if it's any more empty than usual—as if there should be evidence of him packing up, sweeping the corners, forming cubes of matter to throw away methodically in the center of each room, sealing boxes, stacking them. The flat seems clean but little else. Above the bookshelf I notice something I've never seen before. A small portrait, the size of a passport photo. It's connected to the three other small portraits, I can now can see, by a red nylon thread. I wonder if it's new. Instead of packing, he's made a symbolic burial or hanging, something like that, a beware sign for future passersby.

I don't ask if it's new—he wouldn't have given me a straight answer—so I ask what it is.

"An artwork," he says.

Whether it's his or not he does not disclose, though he says he "installed" it with an artist.

"And who are they, the men in the portraits? They seem very familiar to me."

"My four heroes," he says. I can't remember if he smirks or not as he says this, but I can't help myself, and guffaw.

He says "Wwwhat?" drawing out the "w" to make himself sound like a child convicted of something mischievous by his parents. His eyes are shining a bit.

I look away.

I look at the artwork.

I pretend to take it in, to study it as one normally studies artworks; seriously and conscientiously. I think he's looking up at it, too, in those drawn-out minutes, although I can't be sure, because I don't look at him and the view from my peripheral vision is ambiguous. I am sure, though, that as I stared at the artwork in an excuse to let myself think (and I thought furiously, about this strange opaque line he seemed to draw across the world with everything he did), he also thought furiously—this time, I can't indulge him my polite doubt about what was going on inside his head. He was thinking fast, vividly, about me, about who I was, and he was planning something, maybe something for that very evening, for those next moments we'd have.

I catch his eyes when I look back down from the artwork, and he is looking straight at me, and probably already has for a while. Even now that I notice and catch his eyes, he doesn't stop, he continues to look straight at me.

I have no idea what he's seeing.

I look back at him and I see his barbarously ironic mustard Carhartt jacket, which he often wears, looking as stiff and waxed as the day he bought it, like a piece of cardboard that's been wet and then dried, his thinned out neck and head, a nose that seems like a beak only by virtue of the cunning in his eyes.

I look at his face, I'm thinking about this opaque movement he traces. Back then, a few moments ago, as I stared at the artwork, admittedly a little bit scared, I'd fleetingly glimpsed that movement, it had revealed itself to me … But revealed is the wrong word, because if asked to describe it I wouldn't be able to use words, at least not to immediate effect, the movement itself is impossible to see in any way other than abstractly, its logic is like an insistent underwater tug without a face or a name, but somehow I had connected with it.

At least that's what I'm feeling in those moments standing next to him, so close to some very quiet oblivion; as close as you can probably ever get to oblivion without dying shortly after, I think. I realize then that I know him very well, that we are desperately close, him and I, beyond the mediocre surface of events. I realize that there exists between us some ecstasy. I want to be part of his life forever—and it had seemed possible, here, in this empty city, this city that wears a mask that outsiders still believe, in this network of darkness and secrets and silence. It had seemed possible in these moments that no one has figured out how to record—it would have been like a perfect murder, chilling, quiet, without a trace and the tidiest solution.

We're still looking at each other.

He breaks out into a smile, but it slides off the left side of his face and down his shoulder. He doesn't say anything, still looking at me, saying nothing, it feels like a stand-off, but for what? Again I feel dumb and muted, everything in me, months of gagged passions and frantic theorizing desperate to surface, goes flat, loses the chord that would have brought it into articulation.

What can I become with him? Something anonymous? Static? Secret? Sunken?

I realize what I have to do.

Hard-edged piece-of-shit bastard, fucker, asshole.

What's he doing here in Milan? He's never explained it to anyone and whatever he's said is not to be believed. He is in an international quandry. What violence is he plotting? He is flipping the idea of the city upon itself.

    I feel revved up beyond control. I know I'm going nowhere. I wonder if I'll be able to hold on.

I have to leave this city before he does.

ABOUT THE AUTHOR

Lodovico Pignatti Morano was born in London and grew up mostly in Australia. He is the author of *Cinelli: The Art and Design of the Bicycle* (Rizzoli New York, 2012), and editor of *Ideas from Massimo Osti* (Damiani, 2012). He attended Goldsmiths University in London, and moved to Italy in 2009 to work in the cycling industry.